VOLUME I

VOLUME I

**by Marcia Thornton Jones
and
Debbie Dadey**

illustrated by John Steven Gurney

SCHOLASTIC INC.
New York Toronto London Auckland Sydney
Mexico City New Delhi Hong Kong Buenos Aires

The Monsters Next Door, ISBN 0-590-10787-9, text copyright © 1997 by Marcia Thornton Jones
and Debra S. Dadey. Illustrations copyright © 1997 by Scholastic Inc.

Howling at the Hauntlys', ISBN 0-590-10845-X, text copyright © 1998 by Marcia Thornton Jones
and Debra S. Dadey. Illustrations copyright © 1998 by Scholastic Inc.

Vampire Trouble, ISBN 0-590-10846-8, text copyright © 1998 by Marcia Thornton Jones
and Debra S. Dadey. Illustrations copyright © 1998 by Scholastic Inc.

Kilmer's Pet Monster, ISBN 0-590-10847-6, text copyright © 1998 by Marcia Thornton Jones
and Debra S. Dadey. Illustrations copyright © 1998 by Scholastic Inc.

12 11 10 9 8 7 6 5 4 3 2 1   4 5 6 7 8 9/0

Printed in the U.S.A.   40

This edition created exclusively for Barnes & Noble, Inc.
2004 Barnes & Noble Books

ISBN 0-7607-6027-6

First compilation printing, August 2004

minded Annie of a hearse. There was a tall, pale man with red hair wearing a long, black cape with a bloodred button holding it around his neck. The lady seemed normal enough, except for her hair. It stuck up like it was full of electricity. She had on a white doctor's coat, but it was covered with red, green, and purple stains.

The boy had a broad forehead and his hair was cut flat across the top of his head. He only needed bolts on his neck and Annie would have sworn he was Frankenstein's monster she'd seen on a late-night movie. He even wore the monster's ragged jeans and a shirt three sizes too small.

"I'd hate to meet that family in a dark alley," Annie said. "They give me the creeps."

"Speaking of creepy," Ben said, "here comes that monster teacher from school." A red-haired woman in a purple, polka-dotted dress walked down the sidewalk. Mrs. Jeepers taught one of the third-grade classes at Bailey Elementary. All of her students were convinced she was a vampire

3

since she lived in a haunted house and wore a glowing green brooch. Most of the kids at school said the brooch was magic. Ben didn't believe it, but Annie did.

"I'm glad I'm in the other third-grade class," Annie said.

"Mrs. Jeepers must know them," Ben said as Mrs. Jeepers hugged each one of the newcomers before the whole group went inside the house.

Annie stood up from behind the bush. "If they know Mrs. Jeepers," she said, "then

Contents

The Monsters
Next Door

*To my friends
next door Anna Schafer,
Gail Stoltz, Linda Jurgaitis,
Barb Baker, Andrea Marvel, and
Barb Green.—DD*

*To Kathleen and David Salas.
—MTJ*

1

Family from Freaksville

"Those are the weirdest people I've seen in my entire life," Annie whispered to her older brother, Ben. Annie and Ben were hiding behind a bush watching their new neighbors move into the brand-new house next door, 13 Dedman Street.

Ben rolled his eyes. "Can't you take a joke?" he asked, standing up to get a better view. "They're just dressed up for Halloween."

"Halloween is still a week away," Annie said. "These people are a family from Freaksville."

"I think they're cool," Ben said. "And that boy looks about my age."

Annie shuddered and looked at the oddly dressed trio. They were unloading boxes from a long, black station wagon that re-

there is something definitely wrong with them."

"Don't be such a baby," Ben told his sister. "Let's go see what they're doing."

Annie folded her arms in front of her chest. "I am not going to spy in their windows. It's not right."

"Fine," Ben said, "I'll do it without you."

Ben took off toward the house. Annie sighed and followed her brother. "I didn't think you were coming," Ben said.

Annie shrugged. "Somebody has to keep you out of trouble." Together they peeked into a large window in the side of the house. The lady with wild hair opened up a large box marked DUST.

"What kind of crazy people would bring dust with them?" Annie said.

"The kind that throw dust everywhere," Ben said. Annie and Ben watched in disbelief as the lady scattered dust all over the furniture the moving people had carried in.

"That lady is insane," Annie said. "Let's

get out of here before she turns us into giant dust bunnies."

Ben and Annie backed away from the window, but they didn't get far. A firm hand on Annie's shoulder stopped her dead in her tracks.

2
A Sticky Problem

"Aahhh!" Annie screamed.

Ben jumped back, ready to punch a monster in the chin. Instead, he stumbled over a bush and fell down right in the middle of the prickly branches.

A familiar face leaned over Ben and grinned. "Since when do you take naps in bushes?"

Annie grabbed her best friend's arm and giggled. "Jane, you scared us. We thought you were one of the new neighbors."

Jane and Annie had been best friends ever since Ben could remember. That was bad news for Ben since Jane was in his fourth-grade class. Jane pestered him all day at school, and then she and Annie ganged up on him at home.

"Help me up," Ben sputtered. "I think this is a thorn bush."

Jane rubbed her chin and acted like she was thinking very hard. "I'll make you a deal. You tell me what you were doing peeking in that window, and I'll help you up."

Ben took a deep breath. Jane was always trying to make deals.

"I'll make you a deal," Ben said. "You help me out and I won't beat you up."

Jane laughed. "Ben, you might scare all the little kids at school, but I know you're not as tough as you sound."

"Oh yeah? Just wait until I get out of this bush. I'll show you how tough I am." Ben kicked and wiggled until he was free of the sticky bush. The minute Ben stood up he lost his balance and fell back down.

"Not so fast," Jane said, looking down at her friend. "You haven't told me what you were up to."

"I don't have to tell you anything," Ben muttered.

"You do if you want out of that bush,"

Jane said, putting her hands on her hips. "Now, are you going to tell me or not?"

"I'll tell you," Annie offered.

"You be quiet," Ben warned. "Jane doesn't have to know everything."

"I do need to know if you want me to help you," Jane pointed out.

Ben thought about arguing some more, but he didn't like the way one of the branches was poking him in the arm. "This is like getting a booster shot with a tree trunk," he complained. "Okay, I'll tell you."

"Promise to tell the truth?" Jane asked.

"Don't I always?" Ben said.

Annie and Jane laughed. Ben never told the truth if he could help it. Jane held out her hand. "Shake on it," Jane ordered.

"Sure," Ben said with a lopsided grin, but instead of shaking Jane's hand he grabbed it and pulled. Jane landed beside Ben in the sticky bush.

"Oww!" Jane hollered. "That wasn't fair."

Annie giggled. "Of course it wasn't fair. Ben is never fair."

"Stop laughing," Jane begged, "and get me out of here."

"Perhaps I could help," said a strange voice with a thick accent.

Annie stopped laughing and turned around to face the strange voice. She gasped at what she saw.

3

Hauntly Manor Inn

The three friends froze as the new boy came around the corner of the house. He walked like his knees were frozen stiff. Every step with his heavy brown shoes left a deep footprint. When the boy reached the bush, he grabbed Ben's and Jane's arms and pulled. Both flew out of the bush, landing next to the strange kid. Annie noticed that the new neighbor was at least a head taller than Ben.

"Is sitting in the bushes an American custom?" the kid asked.

"N-No," Ben stammered. "Jane scared me and I fell. It's her fault."

"That's me," Jane said, sticking out her hand. Jane's knuckles cracked when the new kid shook her hand. "This is Ben and Annie. Are you from another country?"

12

"I am pleased to meet you," the new boy said. "My name is Kilmer Hauntly. I am from the Transylvanian Alps in Romania. My family and I noticed you watching us through the window. That is a strange way to meet neighbors. But then, everything about America is strange to me."

Annie's face turned red. "We shouldn't have looked in your windows. But we really wanted to meet you."

Kilmer grinned. "Please, do come in. My family wants to meet you, too." Kilmer walked toward the front door.

"Do you think it's safe?" Annie whispered to her brother.

"Of course it's safe," Ben said, but he didn't sound very sure.

Ben, Jane, and Annie followed Kilmer to the front of the house. They already knew the way. The house was brand-new and the kids had explored the empty rooms before the Hauntlys moved in. It was the biggest house on Dedman Street and it still smelled like wet paint.

14

Kilmer stopped just inside the door to pet a black cat perched on a stool.

"What a cute kitty," Annie said. She reached out to pet the cat, but Kilmer stopped her.

"Sparky is not very friendly," he said.

Just then, Sparky's yellow eyes grew round as she stared down the empty hall. She hissed, arched her back, and raced through a door.

Ben laughed. "Sparky looks like she just saw a ghost."

Annie and Jane giggled, but Kilmer didn't even smile. Instead, he led the three kids into the living room. The lady with the stained coat was opening another box that had the word WEBS scribbled on the side. The DUST box was empty and a fine layer of dust covered everything in the room.

"This is my mother, Hilda," Kilmer said.

Kilmer's mother looked like she had been dipped in milk. Her skin was as white as her teeth and her wild hair. "She is a scientist," Kilmer said. Ben, Jane, and Annie

15

all smiled at their new neighbor. "We moved here because she got a job at FATS."

Annie knew that FATS was a big scientific lab at the edge of Bailey City. The initials stood for Federal Aeronautics Technology Station. Annie gulped and wondered what kind of scientist Hilda Hauntly was.

"Your auntie Jeepers was right," Hilda told Kilmer. "She said you would have plenty of friends in Bailey City." Then Hilda called into another room. "Boris, come meet Kilmer's new friends."

Boris Hauntly looked like his feet never touched the floor as he glided into the room, his black cape flowing behind him. Annie gulped when she saw Boris' slime-green eyes.

"What a delicious treat," Boris said, licking his lips. He spoke with the same thick accent as Kilmer and Hilda.

Jane held out her hand. "Welcome to the neighborhood," she said as Boris shook her hand.

Boris grinned so big his pointy eyeteeth

16

showed. Then he spread out his hands and said in a booming voice, "Welcome to Hauntly Manor Inn, a bed-and-breakfast hotel for weary travelers from all over the world."

"Hauntly Manor Inn?" Annie said in a squeaky voice.

Boris nodded. "And you shall be our special guests this Friday evening. We will have a party!"

"Then we must hurry," Hilda said. "This house is not decent for receiving guests."

"Remember to come back Friday," Boris said as he ushered the three kids to the front door, "as soon as the sun sets."

4
Fair and Square

"How about a game?" Jane asked Annie and Ben the next afternoon. Jane carried her old dirty soccer ball into their backyard.

"Let's play boys against girls," Annie said. "We'll beat Ben fair and square."

"Two against one is not fair," Ben argued. "We need another boy." Then he slapped his forehead. "And I know just where to find one."

Ben, Annie, and Jane jogged next door to the Hauntlys'. Ben lifted the tarnished door knocker and let it fall. Moments later, they heard heavy footsteps echoing through Hauntly Manor. The door slowly opened.

Kilmer smiled. "Please," he said in his strange accent, "come in."

Ben shook his head. "Would you like to play soccer?" he asked. "I need you for my team."

Jane laughed. "He'll need more than you," she said. "Ben is the worst player in Bailey City."

"Am not," Ben argued. He patted Kilmer on the shoulder and said to him, "I bet together, we could beat their socks off."

Kilmer frowned. "But I do not know how to play," he told Ben.

"No problem," Ben said. "I'll teach you everything you need to know."

The four kids gathered at the dead end part of Dedman Street and started to play. Kilmer tried to catch up to the ball, but he wasn't used to playing soccer.

Soon, Annie and Jane were winning and Ben got desperate. He side-kicked the ball all the way to Kilmer. Kilmer gave the ball a mighty kick. Ben, Annie, and Jane stopped dead in their tracks when the ball zoomed straight into the goal.

"All right," Ben said, doing a little victory dance. "That's the way to play. Kilmer and I are a great team!"

"It won't do you any good," Jane said, pointing. Kilmer had kicked the ball so hard, it popped. Now the ball was as flat as a pizza.

"That was an old ball anyway," Ben said with a grin. "Next time we'll use my new one."

Annie picked up the flat ball. "This reminds me. Mom said we could decorate our pumpkins today."

"Decorate pumpkins?" Kilmer asked.

"We always paint faces on our pumpkins and make them look really eerie," Annie said.

Kilmer nodded. "That sounds like something my family would enjoy."

"Come on," Ben said. "I'll show you how to make a great painted jack-o'-lantern."

The kids spent the rest of the afternoon decorating pumpkins. When they finished, they admired their work.

Annie's pumpkin had a big grin. Jane's

pumpkin had a crooked frown. Ben's pumpkin was so messy you couldn't tell what it was. But Kilmer's pumpkin looked like something out of a monster movie, complete with pointy fangs.

"That's the scariest pumpkin I've ever seen," Annie said. "How did you think of a face like that?"

Kilmer shrugged. "I just thought about one of my cousins. Maybe he'll come to visit someday." Kilmer walked home to perch his painted jack-o'-lantern on Hauntly Manor's porch.

Annie shuddered. She hoped she'd never see anybody who looked as scary as Kilmer's pumpkin.

5

Halloween

"We're going to Burger Doodle for a milk shake," Annie said after school a few days later. "Do you want to come?" Ben, Annie, and Jane were standing beside the jungle gym with Kilmer.

"Then we're going to play soccer," Ben said. "With you on my side, we can beat the pants off Annie and Jane again."

Kilmer shook his head. "I must do my homework and help make the inn ready." Kilmer looked both ways and crossed Forest Lane. Annie, Ben, and Jane followed him as he turned down Dedman Street.

"You've been going to Bailey Elementary for three whole days," Ben said to Kilmer, "and we've only played soccer once. Don't you think it's time to have some fun?"

Kilmer grinned at Ben. "I am having fun getting ready for the party."

Kilmer's cat, Sparky, was perched on the Hauntly Manor porch railing. Her yellow eyes watched Kilmer wave to the three kids. The cat continued to stare at the kids even after Kilmer disappeared inside the front door.

"I can't wait until Friday," Jane said. "I already have my costume. I'm going to be a ghost."

Annie grinned. "I'm going to be a princess. I just have to finish making my crown."

"Do you think the Hauntlys know that Friday is Halloween?" Jane asked.

"Of course they do," Ben said. "That's why they're having a party."

"Strange," Annie said. "Kilmer never mentioned Halloween."

"That's not the only strange thing," Jane said. "Have you noticed Hauntly Manor lately?"

"What about it?" Annie asked.

"Well," Jane said slowly, "when the Hauntlys moved in last weekend that house was brand-new. Now look at it. Houses don't turn old that fast."

Jane was right. Two shutters were lopsided and a jagged crack reached across one of the living room windows. The railing leading up to the porch was falling apart and the tree in the front yard had died. Even the grass had turned from bright green to a sickly shade of dirty brown.

"This place is creepy," Ben admitted.

"Worse," Jane said. "It looks downright haunted!"

"Don't be silly," Annie said. "Houses have to be old to have ghosts."

"Unless," Ben said, looking at the black cat on the porch, "ghosts moved in."

"With vampires," Jane added, "and mad scientists."

Annie adjusted her backpack and looked at Jane. "What are you talking about?"

"You have to admit the Hauntlys are unusual," Ben said.

"So are you," Annie said. "But that doesn't make you a goblin."

"Remember Hilda?" Jane argued. "She's as pale as a ghost and she always wears that lab coat with weird stains."

"Boris' eyeteeth make him look like Dracula's cousin," Ben added. "After all, they are from Transylvania. Isn't that where Dracula is from?"

"What about Kilmer?" Annie asked.

Jane sat her backpack on the sidewalk. "Maybe Kilmer's an experiment Hilda cooked up in her lab."

"You're crazy," Annie said. "The Hauntlys seem strange to us because they're new to this country."

"Then how do you explain a brand-new house turning into a haunted house?" Jane asked.

Annie laughed. "It's for the party," she said. "Friday is Halloween."

Just then, Sparky arched her back and

hissed. Then she darted around the house as if a monster were chasing her tail.

Jane took a deep breath. "I hope you're right," she told Annie. "Or we're in for the Halloween surprise of our lives."

6

Monster Movies

On Halloween evening Ben, Annie, and Jane walked with Kilmer to meet a group of other Bailey School kids at the mall.

Annie wore a long pink dress with a sparkling crown. Jane had on a bedsheet with two holes in it for her to see through. Ben had wrapped himself in white rags to look like a mummy. Kilmer looked like he always did. He wore heavy brown shoes, jeans, and a shirt that was too small.

"I can't wait until your party," Annie told Kilmer.

"We'll go right after trick or treating at the mall," Jane said. "It'll be dark by then."

"I am sure it will be fun," Kilmer said to his new friends. "But why did you tell me to bring this pillowcase?" He held up a case as black as the night sky.

"For all your treats," Annie told him.

"You probably always used plastic bags," Ben said. "But I learned a long time ago that pillowcases hold more loot."

A large group of Bailey School kids were already at the mall. The Bailey Elementary principal, Mr. Davis, was dressed up as Humpty Dumpty.

Kilmer smiled when he saw all the costumes. "Ah," he said, "this reminds me so much of my home in Transylvania."

The big group of kids went to every shop in the mall. Each store gave treats to the kids.

"Mega Ghost Bubble Balls," Ben hollered, "my favorite!"

"I'll make you a deal," Jane said. "I'll trade you my Mega Balls for your suckers."

"It's a deal," Ben said, "if you throw in your licorice and chocolate-covered pretzels."

"Fine," Jane said. "I don't like those anyway."

After Ben, Annie, and Jane finished trading, the four kids hurried to the center of the mall. They got there just in time for the costume contest. Annie giggled when Kilmer won first prize for best costume, but Ben didn't laugh. He was mad because Kilmer's bag had more treats in it. In fact, Kilmer had more treats than anybody.

"Don't be mad," Kilmer told him. "You can have mine. I really do not like candy."

"You don't like candy?" a girl named Liza asked. Liza and her friends Howie, Melody, and Eddie were in Mrs. Jeepers' third-grade class at Bailey Elementary.

Kilmer shook his head. "The treats my mother makes are much better. You will see when you come to my house. You are all invited."

"But we can't go yet," Liza's friend Eddie griped. "The theater is showing monster cartoons."

Kilmer smiled before walking away. "Meet me at my house after the cartoons. We are planning a great party!"

It was dark when the movie let out. The

kids hurried down Forest Lane. As soon as they turned onto Dedman Street a chilling wind sent dead leaves scurrying at their feet. Jane and Annie glanced over their shoulders to make sure no monsters lurked in the shadows.

Annie looked up at the bare tree branches. They reminded her of long bony fingers, blowing in the wind. Annie expected one of the branches to grab her any minute. But the branches didn't grab Annie, they grabbed Ben.

"You're coming undone." Annie giggled as one of the branches snagged Ben's costume. A long piece of Ben's white rag fluttered in the wind.

"Fix it," Ben ordered Annie.

"I'd be glad to tie you up," Jane interrupted. She hurried to fix Ben's costume before the wind unraveled it all.

When Ben stopped in front of the Hauntly Manor Inn, Melody gulped and said, "Is that where Kilmer lives?"

The group of Bailey School kids peered

up at the black windows of Hauntly Manor. A loose shutter banged against the paint-chipped wall and wind moaned through the dead tree branches in the front yard. Dozens of eerie jack-o'-lanterns flickered on the Hauntlys' front porch. Annie was sure she heard a werewolf howling in the distance.

Jane nodded. "I told you their house was creepy."

"It's worse than creepy," Howie said. "It looks like something out of the monster movie we just saw."

Annie pointed to the dark windows. "It doesn't look like anybody is home," she said.

"They must be home," Jane told her. "The Hauntlys have been planning this party for days."

"It looks quiet," Ben said. "Deathly quiet."

"Maybe we shouldn't go in there," Liza said. Annie nodded in agreement.

"Are you out of your mind?" Eddie asked. "Kilmer said his mother's treats are better than candy. I'm not about to miss out on them."

"Then you're not afraid to go first?" Melody asked.

"I'm not afraid," Eddie said, "if Ben's not afraid."

Eddie and Ben looked at each other. It was a known fact that Eddie and Ben were always trying to prove who was the toughest kid in Bailey City.

"I'm not afraid," Ben told him.

"Me neither," Eddie said. But Eddie and Ben didn't move until Jane gave them a shove.

The group of kids slowly followed Ben and Eddie up the creaking steps to the Hauntly Hotel. Together, Ben and Eddie lifted the heavy metal knocker and let it fall against the wooden door. A loud knock echoed within.

Slowly, the door creaked open.

7
Beethoven's Ghost

Boris Hauntly sent chills up the kids' backs when he opened the door. "Welcome to Hauntly Manor Inn," he said in a deep voice.

Annie took one look at Boris as the full moon shone on his slime-green eyes and almost fainted. "I'm not going in there," Annie whispered to Jane.

Jane nodded. "You're right," she said. "Let's get out of here." But before they could run, the whole group of kids squeezed through the door, pushing Jane and Annie inside Hauntly Manor. Boris closed the heavy door with a loud thud.

"Trapped," Annie whispered with a gulp.

"Wow," Ben said, "we like what you've done with the place."

Boris smiled, showing his huge pointy eyeteeth. "Yes, it feels very homey now."

The kids looked around. It looked anything but homey to them. The inside of the house was painted red, bloodred. A thick layer of dust covered heavy antique furniture and cobwebs clung in every corner. Huge candelabras filled with fat, dripping candles were the only light in the spooky house. As Boris showed them into the living room, Annie felt like she was in her worst nightmare.

"Phe-ew!" Eddie said rudely. "It smells like something died in here."

Liza squeezed Eddie's shoulder. "Be quiet," she whispered. "Don't you know who that is?"

"Of course I do," Eddie snapped. "That's Kilmer's dad."

Liza squeezed Eddie's arm so hard he jumped. "That's Boris Hauntly. He's Mrs. Jeepers' brother. We met him at Mrs. Jeepers' family reunion."

41

Eddie looked at Boris and nodded. At the reunion, Eddie and his friends Liza, Melody, and Howie had all thought Boris was a vampire bat. Now he was living here in Bailey City. Eddie pulled his costume up over his neck.

Annie jumped and grabbed Ben's arm when a huge pump organ in the corner of the room started playing loud, creepy music. "Oh my gosh," she told Ben, "there's nobody playing the organ."

Ben looked. Sure enough, the keys were being pressed down, but the organ bench was empty. "Maybe the ghost of Hauntly Manor likes Beethoven," Ben joked.

But Ben wasn't smiling when Hilda swept into the room and greeted the children. Her eyes looked just as wild as her spiky hair. When she shook Ben's hand, Ben felt like he was touching a dead woman. Hilda's hand was bony and cold, stone cold.

The entire group of kids huddled together in the middle of the living room, staring at the strange pictures on the wall,

when a loud clomping noise sounded over the organ music.

Clomp. Clomp. CLOMP.

"What's that?" Annie asked Ben nervously.

Ben gulped. "I don't know. But it's getting closer."

8

Burying Things

Kilmer stomped into the room with his heavy shoes. "Welcome!" he told the kids. "Would you like a tour of Hauntly Manor?"

Annie shook her head, but no one noticed. Kilmer grabbed her hand and dragged her into the hall. Kilmer's grip was so strong, Annie had no choice but to follow him. Ben and Jane hurried to catch up while the other kids gathered around the organ in the living room.

"Let me show you the conservatory," Kilmer said.

"What's a conservation?" Ben asked Jane.

"He said conservatory, noodle brain," Jane told Ben.

"So, since you're so smart, what's a conservatory?" Ben asked.

Jane shrugged. "I think it's a place to put your bottles and cans for recycling."

Kilmer led the group into a glass room. The glass walls were lined with hundreds of clay pots filled with withered brown plants. In the center of the room lay four long flower beds piled with mounds of rich black soil. "How nice to have a room just to grow plants," Annie told Kilmer.

Kilmer nodded. "My father is an active gardener. He loves burying things in the

soil. He even brought this special dirt all the way from Transylvania."

Ben poked Jane in the arm. "I don't see any recycling bins in here."

Jane stuck out her tongue at Ben. "Maybe Boris is recycling dead bodies instead of paper," she said softly.

Annie looked at the dying plants. "I'm sure the plants will be beautiful once they've recovered from moving," she told Kilmer.

Kilmer looked at Annie in a funny way. "My father thinks they are beautiful just like this."

Annie didn't say anything, she just followed Kilmer into the next room. "This is my mother's laboratory," Kilmer explained.

"Cool," Ben said as he looked around the cluttered room. Test tubes of every size and shape lined black countertops. A nearby beaker oozed with thick green bubbles.

Ben reached out his hand to grab one of the test tubes, but Kilmer stopped him. "Don't touch that," Kilmer warned. "My mother has some very strong chemicals in here. There's no telling what they might do to you."

Ben pulled his hand back and nodded. Jane tapped Ben on the shoulder. "I'll make you a deal," Jane said. "You drink one of those and I won't bother you for a week."

"No way," Ben said. "I might be turned into some kind of monster."

Jane giggled. "You couldn't be any worse of a monster than you already are."

"You're about as funny as bat poop," Ben said, rolling his eyes at Jane.

Jane and Ben had to hurry as Kilmer took Annie out of the laboratory. Annie still heard the organ playing in the living room, but she heard something else, too. It was a low growling sound.

"What's that funny noise?" she asked Kilmer.

"I hear nothing unusual," Kilmer told her.

The growling grew louder. "I didn't know you had a dog," Annie said.

"A dog? Sparky would never allow us to have a dog. Now, here's the kitchen," continued Kilmer. Then he led them into the strangest room they'd ever seen.

9
Eyeballs

Jane gasped. Annie whimpered and grabbed Ben's arm. The rest of the kids had left the living room and were huddled in a corner of the kitchen. They were staring at Boris with wide eyes. Boris stood in front of a huge door of an iron stove. He was using a sharp poker to stoke up flames. Fire shot up all around him, making him look like he was on fire. In fact, the red painted walls made the whole room look like it was on fire. Gray smoke billowed out of a black cauldron sitting on top of the ancient stove.

"The stove must be a bazillion years old," Annie blurted.

Kilmer nodded. "It has been in my family since the beginning of time."

Boris used a long wooden spoon to stir whatever was in the cauldron. Then he

turned and smiled at the crowd of kids. Jane couldn't help noticing his pointy eye-teeth.

"You're just in time for a special Hauntly Manor Inn treat," Boris told the kids. "Who's hungry?"

Eddie's and Ben's hands shot into the air. "I'm starved," Ben yelled.

Kilmer pulled Ben over to the stove. "My dad cooked up something extra special for my new friends. You can be the first to sample some of these great broiled lizard tongues."

Boris held out a tarnished silver tray loaded with red and pink strips. Ben took one look at the tongues and lost his appetite.

"Go ahead," Kilmer told Ben, "they're delicious."

Ben gulped. "That's okay. I'll let Eddie go first."

Eddie frowned. "What else do you have to eat?" he asked.

"We have a feast," Boris told the kids. He

53

waved his hand toward a huge wooden table.

"All of my favorites!" Kilmer said, pointing to several trays. "Roasted skeleton knuckles, fried rat claws, and boiled buzzard eyeballs."

The kids looked at Eddie. He didn't move. They looked at Ben. His face was as white as his mummy costume. Just then a strange sound came from upstairs. It sounded like huge claws scratching on the floor above them.

"W-What's that?" Annie stammered.

"That's probably the skeletons coming to get their knuckles back," Ben joked.

But nobody laughed because just then the howling began. "Let's get out of here!" Melody screamed.

The kids dashed away from Kilmer and Boris, pushing Jane, Annie, and Ben with them. They didn't stop running until they reached the shadows of the dead tree.

"Why did you run?" Jane asked.

"Didn't you hear that monster?" Liza whimpered. "It was coming to get us."

Ben laughed. "This is Halloween, you pumpkinhead. That was just a spooky tape."

"What about the rat claws, skeleton knuckles, and buzzard eyeballs?" Howie said. "There's something very strange going on here."

"Of course there is," Jane said. "After all, it is Halloween."

"Halloween at the Hauntlys is anything but normal," Eddie said.

"You guys are crazy," Ben said.

"Not as crazy as you," Melody said. "I'm going for help."

Then the gang of kids raced down Dedman Street, leaving Annie, Ben, and Jane standing alone in the dark under the dead tree.

10

Nothing but Trouble

"We have to do something," Ben told Jane and Annie. They huddled under the dead tree in the Hauntly Manor yard. A full moon cast eerie shadows across the lawn.

"I plan to," Jane said. "I'm going home and eating candy until I'm sick."

Annie grabbed Jane's arm. "How can you think of eating after seeing buzzard eyeballs and rat claws?"

"Those weren't real," Jane argued. "I'm sure they were just for Halloween."

"Eddie thought they were real enough to go for help," Annie said. "I bet they'll run the Hauntlys out of town."

"We can't let that happen to Kilmer," Ben said. "He's the only other boy on this block."

Jane tugged off her ghost costume and stuffed it into her bag of candy. "Who cares about Kilmer?" she said. "The two of you together are trouble anyway."

Ben grinned. "Exactly. I'm not about to let the best thing that happened to Dedman Street get chased out of town by a little squirt like Eddie."

"You're going to be in trouble if you mess with Eddie," Annie said.

"Eddie doesn't scare me," Ben said. "Besides, with the Hauntlys on our side we'll never have to worry again."

"But what about Boris and Hilda?" Jane asked. "I don't like having monsters for neighbors."

"You shouldn't call Boris and Hilda monsters," Annie said. "They may be a little different, but that doesn't mean they should be run out of town."

"Annie's right for once," Ben said. "And it's up to us to help them. Come here and I'll tell you my plan."

Jane and Annie gathered close to Ben,

but before Ben could say another word Boris glided out the front door. Hilda and Kilmer followed close behind.

"Ben," Kilmer called. "Please come back and have some treats."

Hilda put her long bony fingers on Annie's arm. "Is there a problem?" Hilda asked Annie. "Everyone left so suddenly."

"There's a problem," Ben blurted out, "a big problem. Let's get inside before some-body sees us and we'll tell you all about it."

"Can't you shut that racket up?" Ben asked Kilmer about the loud organ music as everyone settled into the dusty living room. Instantly, the organ stopped playing and Hauntly Manor became deathly still.

"How'd you do that?" Annie asked softly.

Kilmer smiled. "We have a very talented organ."

Ben wanted to ask Kilmer about the organ, but he knew he didn't have a mo-ment to waste. Ben told the Hauntlys all about Halloween.

When Ben finished, Boris scratched his head. "Explain this again," Boris asked Ben.

"Every year kids dress up as monsters and ghosts," Ben said.

"And princesses," Annie interrupted.

Ben frowned at Annie and continued. "It's a chance to pretend to be whatever we want to be. But the best part is getting lots and lots of treats."

"You mean like boiled eyeballs and roasted skeleton knuckles?" Kilmer asked.

"No, no," Jane said. "In Bailey City, we like candy and junk food. Nobody wants healthy stuff for Halloween."

Hilda Hauntly shook her head. "What a strange custom."

"We must find a costume," Boris told his family, "before the others return."

Jane held up her hand. "No, believe me. You're fine just the way you are."

"We need to get some of this junk food and candy for our guests," Hilda said.

"You can use some of my candy," Annie

said. She dumped her candy onto the thick black rug.

Jane dug through Annie's candy bars, suckers, and candy corn. "This won't work. Not a single thing looks like buzzard eyeballs or rat claws," she pointed out.

"Listen," Annie said. "I think I hear Eddie and the rest of the kids outside. We'd better think of something and fast."

Jane pawed through her own bag of candy. "I don't have anything that will work, either."

Boom. Boom. Boom. "They're banging on the door," Annie said with a gulp. "What are we going to do?"

Ben darted toward the kitchen with his bag of candy. "Let them in," he yelled over his shoulder. "Leave the rest to me."

11

Trick or Treat?

Boom. Boom. Boom.

"Okay," Ben said as he came out of the kitchen. Ben, still dressed in his mummy costume, held a huge tray. "Open the front door."

"Maybe you shouldn't," Annie said. "They sound awfully mad."

"Don't worry about a thing," Ben told them. "I have it all under control."

The door creaked as Boris slowly pulled it open. "Happy Halloween," he said in his strange Transylvanian accent.

The crowd gasped and stepped back — everybody, that is, but Principal Davis. "Please come in and have some treats," Hilda said politely.

Eddie peeked from behind Principal

Davis. "Go ahead and ask them about the eyeballs."

Ben grinned. "Sure, we have plenty of eyeballs and rat claws, too." And then, Ben, the mummy, stepped in front of Boris and held up the tray. It was piled high with white bubblegum balls and chocolate-covered pretzels.

"What about the broiled lizard tongues?" Melody asked.

Annie pointed to a mound of long stringy licorice. "Here they are. Don't you want some?"

Eddie folded his arms over his chest. "You guys are tricking us."

"We're just trying to give you a treat," Jane laughed. "I'll make you a deal. You have a treat and we'll never tell anyone what a big chicken you were this Halloween at the Hauntlys'."

Ben gave the tray to Kilmer and flapped his wings. "*Bawk. Bawk. Bawk.*"

Principal Davis scratched his bald head.

"I think you children have had enough excitement for one night. I know I have." Principal Davis disappeared down Dedman Street after apologizing to the Hauntlys.

The rest of the kids stared at the Hauntlys. "You're not getting away with this," Eddie said.

"Oh no?" Ben asked with a smile.

Just then the organ blasted out a haunting melody, and a piercing howl echoed from the attic of Hauntly Manor.

Two girls screamed and Eddie's face turned as white as Ben's mummy costume.

"Let's get out of here while we still can!" Liza screamed.

12

One Too Many Monsters

The whole group of kids raced down Dedman Street, while Ben and Kilmer laughed.

"That was pretty cool," Ben said to Kilmer. "How'd you get the organ to play?"

Kilmer just smiled. "It's an old family secret," he told his new friends. "We have lots of them."

"Whew," Annie told Jane and Ben when they left the Hauntlys'. "That was close."

"I can't believe you were going to give your candy to Eddie," Jane told Ben.

Annie agreed. "You like candy more than cartoons. You must have really wanted to help Kilmer."

"It's nice having someone to play soccer with," Ben said. "Besides, it was cool when the Hauntlys scared the other kids. I like having the Hauntlys on our side."

Jane shrugged. "It figures that Ben would be the only kid in Bailey City to make friends with a Frankenstein monster. After all, Ben is part monster himself."

Ben held out his arms in front of him like a mummy and walked with stiff legs toward Jane. "I am a monster," Ben said in his creepiest voice.

"I think there are too many monsters on Dedman Street," Jane said. "But I can take care of that."

She snatched a tattered end of Ben's costume and pulled hard. With a little shove from Annie, Ben twirled around and around. His rags unraveled and fell to the ground.

Annie giggled. "That's one less monster around here. But what are we going to do about having the Hauntlys for neighbors? Jane was right about them. I don't know if I'll like having monsterlike people living next door."

"You better get used to it," Ben warned. "I don't think they're going anywhere. Didn't Boris say he was making their house into a bed-and-breakfast?"

"That's right," Annie said. "But who would stay at a monster motel?"

Jane gulped. "Monsters, that's who. Lots and lots of monsters."

Just then the clouds drifted over the full moon and the kids found themselves in total darkness. Wind rattled through bare tree branches, and a howl from the Hauntlys' attic cut through the night.

"We may be in trouble," Annie said. "Big trouble."

Howling at
the Hauntlys'

1

Howling

"That looks silly," Ben told his little sister, Annie.

Annie finished making a raisin smile below her snowman's carrot nose and walnut eyes. "This is what a snowman should look like," she said.

Ben laughed. "Your snowman has no personality. You should make one like mine."

Annie looked at her brother's two-headed snowman. One head had a giant eye in the middle. The other head looked like it was screaming. "Your snowman belongs next door," Annie told him.

Ben and Annie looked at the big house next to theirs. A few months ago, the house had been brand-new. Then the Hauntly family moved in. Now, a loose shutter swayed in the cold wind and most of the windows

had jagged cracks. A lopsided sign hung in the front yard under a dead tree. It said: HAUNTLY MANOR INN. Hauntly Manor looked like something out of a horror movie, and so did the Hauntlys.

Boris Hauntly had slime-green eyes and pointy eyeteeth. He was a dead ringer for Dracula's cousin. His wife, Hilda, always wore a white lab coat covered with strange stains. In fact, Ben and Annie were sure their new neighbors were monsters from Transylvania.

Annie pulled her coat tight. "You know, I think there might be a guest staying at the inn."

"Don't be silly, slush brains." Ben laughed. "There hasn't been a single visitor since the Hauntlys moved in."

"Didn't you hear that howling last night?" Annie asked. "It came from the Hauntlys' backyard."

Ben didn't answer Annie because the door to Hauntly Manor Inn swung open and Kilmer Hauntly stepped out on the porch.

77

Kilmer was in Ben's class at school, but Kilmer was not a regular fourth-grader. He was very tall, so tall his torn jeans didn't reach all the way to his ankles. Kilmer's hair was cut flat across the top of his head, and he reminded Annie of Frankenstein's monster.

Just before Kilmer closed the front door of Hauntly Manor Inn, his cat, Sparky, darted between his legs. Sparky's black fur went in every direction and she looked like she drank coffee instead of milk. She jumped up on the porch railing. As soon as she saw Annie and Ben, Sparky arched her back and hissed. She leaped off the porch and darted around the corner of the house.

Kilmer waved to Annie and Ben then kicked through the snow until he stood in front of Ben's snowman. "What is this?" Kilmer asked.

Ben patted his two-headed snowman's belly. "This is my newest creation," he said. "Annie thinks it looks like a monster."

Kilmer studied the snowman and finally shook his head. "No, I do not know anyone who looks like that. But it is a fine-looking snowman."

"That's what I think," Ben said with a laugh. "Annie is just crazy."

"I am not," Annie argued.

"Yes, you are," Ben told her. Then he rolled his eyes and looked at Kilmer. "She even thought she heard weird noises coming from your backyard last night."

Kilmer shook his head. "I heard nothing unusual."

"Of course not," Ben said, "because the only unusual nutcase on Dedman Street is Annie."

Annie narrowed her eyes. "You better take that back," she said. "Or else."

"Or else what?" Ben asked, his hands on his hips. Annie didn't answer because just then a snowball smacked Ben on the back of his head.

"Bingo!" Jane yelled. Jane lived down the street and was in the same class as Ben and Kilmer.

"You've done it now," Ben yelled. "This is war. Snowball war!"

Before Ben could throw a snowball at Jane, Annie grabbed his arm. "Shh," she warned. "I hear something."

Ben pulled his arm away. "That old trick isn't going to work. You're just trying to give Jane time to run."

"No, I'm not," Annie said. "I really do hear something very strange."

"I hear it, too," Jane said. "It sounds like it's coming from Kilmer's backyard."

The three kids looked at Kilmer. Kilmer shook his head. "I hear nothing unusual," he said.

Ben stood very still so he could listen. "Wait," he said. "The girls might be right."

"Maybe Sparky is in trouble," Annie said.

"There's only one way to find out," Ben said. Without waiting for his friends, Ben took off running toward the back of Hauntly Manor Inn. What he found was hairy, but it was definitely not a cat.

2
Cousin Hauntly

When Kilmer, Annie, and Jane rounded the corner of Hauntly Manor, they found a huge hairy creature pawing through the snow near the screened-in porch. If he hadn't been wearing torn jeans and an old plaid shirt, Jane would've been sure that he was a giant wolf burying a bone.

Kilmer smiled. "It is just my cousin," he told Annie, Ben, and Jane. "His nickname is Fang. He flew in from Transylvania yesterday. He is Hauntly Manor Inn's first guest." Kilmer patted his cousin on the back.

When Kilmer's cousin faced them, Jane gasped and Annie took a giant step back.

Kilmer was different-looking, but the kids were used to him. They weren't used to Fang, though. Fang stood a full head taller than Kilmer and was several years

82

older. Fang was the hairiest kid they had ever seen. He had thick brown hair that came down to a point on his forehead, but that wasn't all. He also had hair on his knuckles and Annie noticed hair peeking out from under his shirtsleeves. There was even hair sticking out from under his jeans and all over his bare feet.

Fang smiled, showing his long yellow canine teeth. "I am happy to meet Kilmer's friends," he said. His voice was rough and sounded like growling.

"We heard something," Annie said. "We thought Sparky might be in trouble."

For a minute, Jane was sure Fang snarled. Then he laughed, only it didn't sound like laughing. It sounded like howling. "I didn't see Kilmer's cat. Believe me, you'd know if I did." Fang licked his lips. "I'd be glad to hunt for the cat. There's not much else to do around here."

Ben grinned. "How about having a snowball fight?" he suggested. "Boys against girls?"

Annie held up her hand. "That's not fair. There are more boys than girls."

Ben nodded. "I know. Before Kilmer moved to Dedman Street, I was always out-numbered. It's about time the boys had the advantage."

"Two girls can beat three boys any day of the week," Jane said as she launched a handful of snow at Ben's face.

Ben ran for a big pile of snow. "War!" he yelled to Kilmer and Fang.

Kilmer and Ben threw dozens of snow-balls at the girls, but Fang was a machine. He jumped down in the snow and quickly scratched up dozens of balls. He hopped up and pelted the girls with the balls. Every time Fang made a direct hit, he would tilt his head back to howl in delight. Fang howled a lot. It gave Annie the chills.

There was no way Annie and Jane could make snowballs fast enough. It looked like they were doomed to lose the snowball war. Just as Jane was ready to call a truce, a snowball sailed over her and landed right

on Kilmer's flat head. Another snowball smacked Ben on the arm. Three more snowballs sailed at the boys like missiles on a battlefield.

"Look out!" Ben yelled. "It's an invasion!"

3
Monster Attack

Kilmer's parents, Boris and Hilda, swooped up beside Annie and Jane. "How about a little help?" Boris asked.

Jane nodded while Hilda launched a snowball right into Ben's head. Boris smiled, showing his pointy eyeteeth, and tossed a ball toward Fang. Annie shivered a bit when she saw Boris' teeth, but she forgot all about it when they started winning the snowball fight.

"Your parents are smearing us!" Ben yelled to Kilmer. Ever since Boris and Hilda joined the fight, the boys were getting hit from the left and right. "I've never seen parents get into a snowball fight like your parents," Ben said.

Kilmer smiled. "I know. Aren't they great?"

"There's nothing great about losing," Ben grumbled.

Fang didn't say anything. He was busy launching three snowballs at once. One hit Boris on the shoulder. Fang tilted his head back and howled.

Kilmer ducked when another snowball whizzed by his cheek. "We were beating the girls. They needed the help."

"It's not fair," Ben said. "Your mom and dad are helping them mash us into slush." Ben quickly launched a snowball toward Jane. Kilmer threw one, too.

Jane dodged the snowball and it hit Kilmer's mom instead. Hilda threw back her head of wild hair and laughed. She looked at Boris and smiled. "This is wonderful. I wish we could have snow every day of the year."

Boris smiled, showing his pointy eye-teeth. His slime-green eyes flashed as he tossed his long black cape onto the ground. "Enjoy it while you can, my dear," Boris said. "It soon will melt."

Hilda nodded at Boris and didn't notice Fang's snowball coming straight for her. BLAM! The snowball hit her right in the mouth.

"That's it for me!" Hilda shouted.

Ben, Kilmer, and Fang ran up to Hilda. "Aunt Hilda, are you all right?" Fang asked.

Hilda nodded and brushed the snow off her pale face. "I am fine," Hilda said to the kids, "but I imagine you are getting hungry. How about a rare calves' liver treat?"

"Bloody good!" Fang yelled, licking his lips.

Annie's stomach did a flip-flop and Jane shook her head. "No, thanks," Jane said. "I'd better work on my science project."

"Me, too," Ben said quickly.

"I promised to help Jane," Annie added as Boris and Hilda went inside Hauntly Manor Inn.

"Since when do you want to do homework?" Jane asked Ben.

"Since never," Ben said. "I just wasn't hungry for raw meat."

"I like doing homework," Kilmer said. "In fact, I will hurry to finish my science project after our snack. Fang said he would help me."

Annie, Jane, and Ben watched Fang and Kilmer disappear inside the inn. Then Jane poked Ben in the arm. "We'd really better work on our science projects," she told Ben. "They're due on Monday."

Ben groaned as the three kids walked back to Ben and Annie's house. "I'd rather crack walnuts with my teeth," he told Jane. "There's something weird about kids who like to do homework."

"Nobody could be as weird as Fang," Jane said. "He's as hairy as my dad's hairbrush."

"He can't help having a lot of hair," Annie said. "Maybe it runs in his family."

"Maybe," Jane said, "if he comes from a family of hairy monsters that eat raw meat for snacks and howl like wolves."

"Very funny—" Annie started to say.

But she was interrupted by loud howling that sent cold chills up her spine.

4

Serious Trouble

Annie huddled close to Jane. "There's only one thing that howls like that," Jane whispered. "A wolf!"

Annie gasped, but Ben laughed out loud. "There aren't any wolves in Bailey City," he told her.

Jane shook her head. "This is no ordinary wolf," she said. "I'm talking about a werewolf. And his name is Fang Hauntly."

Ben laughed so hard he sat down in the snow. "Then I'm the Abominable Snowman."

"Ben's right," Annie told her best friend. "Just because Kilmer's cousin is different, it doesn't mean he's a wolf. Besides, there are no such things as werewolves."

"But there are airheads," Ben said. "And you're the most famous of them all!" With

that, Ben tossed a snowball at Jane. Jane was too fast for him and she dodged the snowball. She quickly packed another one and it zoomed back to hit Ben on the head.

Ben jumped up and pointed at Jane. "You're asking for it," he warned her.

"And who is going to give it to me?" Jane said with a laugh.

"Me," Ben said, "with Kilmer and his cousin. We're going to challenge you to a rematch!" Ben stomped all the way to the Hauntlys' front door.

"You better not go in there," Jane warned. "That raw meat probably just made Fang hungrier. He'll gnaw your bones for dessert."

Ben ignored Jane and knocked on the front door of Hauntly Manor Inn.

Boris opened the front door and let Ben inside. Annie thought Boris' long cape made him look just like a vampire. Annie shivered. "If Fang really is a werewolf, Ben could be in trouble," she said. "Serious trouble."

"So?" Jane said.

"Ben is my brother," Annie told her. "I can't let him become a werewolf snack without trying to save him."

Jane shrugged. "He isn't my brother," she pointed out.

"But you're my best friend," Annie said. "So you have to help me."

Jane sighed and followed Annie back to Hauntly Manor. "I guess you're right. But if you ever tell anyone at school that I saved Ben, I'll deny it!"

"Don't worry," Annie said, knocking on the Hauntlys' door. "I won't tell anyone. Besides, they would never believe me!"

"So nice to see you again," Boris said in his Transylvanian accent as the door creaked open. "Won't you come in?"

The deep red button at Boris' throat looked like a giant drop of blood and his skin was white like the snow. The black cape swirled around Boris' legs, hiding his feet from view, as he led the girls deep into

the darkness of Hauntly Manor. Annie was sure Boris floated instead of walked.

Boris stopped in the doorway of the living room. The walls were painted bloodred and an ancient organ sat in the corner. A thick layer of dust covered everything. "Please, sit down while I whip up a special snack for you." Boris pointed to the velvet couch with legs that looked like claws.

Annie shook her head. "We just came to get Ben," she told Boris.

Boris nodded. "Ben went to find Kilmer and Fang."

"Is it okay if we look for him?" Jane asked.

"Of course," Boris told her. "But . . . do be careful."

"Be careful of what?" Annie asked. But Boris had already disappeared down the dark hallway.

"This place gives me the creeps," Jane said. "It reminds me of a scary movie."

Annie nodded. "I keep thinking something is going to jump out at me from a corner."

"Or grab my ankles," Jane said. Both girls looked at the giant claw feet of the couch and took a giant step away from it.

"Come on," Annie said. "If we're going to save Ben, we'd better hurry."

Together, the girls walked down the hall. Cobwebs hung from corners and a door at the end of the long hall slammed shut. Jane pointed. "Ben must be down there."

"What if he isn't?" Annie asked. "What if

Kilmer's flea-bitten cousin is waiting for us?"

Jane took a deep breath. "Just be ready to run." Together, the girls inched their way down the dark hallway. Step-by-step, closer they came, until they were halfway down the hall.

Annie and Jane never made it to the end of the hallway. As they passed a dark doorway, two hands reached out and grabbed their shoulders.

5
Caught

Annie started to scream, but a hand slapped over her mouth. "Shh," a voice warned. "Don't let them hear you."

"Ben!" Annie hissed. "What are you doing? You scared us to death!"

"You shouldn't be hiding in Hauntly Manor," Jane told him.

Ben pulled Annie and Jane into the shadows. "I wasn't hiding," Ben said. "I was looking around. And I saw something . . . something unusual."

"Did you see Cousin Hauntly turning into a werewolf?" Jane asked.

Ben shook his head. "I haven't seen Kilmer and his cousin at all. But I did find Dr. Hauntly. She's cooking up something."

Annie and Jane knew all about the Hauntlys' strange treats. Boris and the rest of the Hauntlys had tried to give them skeleton knuckles and lizard tongues on Halloween.

Annie patted her brother on the arm. "Don't worry," she said. "You don't have to eat any of it."

"That's not the kind of cooking I'm talking about," Ben hissed.

"Then what are you jabbering about?" Jane asked.

Ben pulled them deeper into the dark hall. "Come with me and I'll show you."

"Sneaking around someone's house isn't polite," Annie said.

"Polite isn't in my vocabulary," Ben said, stopping in front of a closed door.

Gray mist oozed from beneath the door and when Jane sniffed she smelled something like cotton candy. "Whatever Dr. Hauntly is cooking, it smells good," Jane said.

"It's better than good," Ben said. "Look."

Ben slowly turned the doorknob to crack open the door. The three kids leaned close to peak into Dr. Hauntly's laboratory. Hilda Hauntly was a scientist at FATS, the Federal Aeronautics Technology Station. They knew she had a laboratory in Hauntly Manor, but they had never seen her working there.

Hilda stood in front of a long black counter. The counter was cluttered with test tubes and beakers. Some of the glass containers had green liquid, a few of them bubbled, and three of them had smoke rolling off the top. Hilda wasn't paying any attention to them. She was busy scribbling notes on a piece of paper. Then she carefully measured out a spoonful of creamy white stuff and dumped it into a metal bowl.

"Watch this," Ben whispered. "This is the good part."

Hilda flipped a switch and the bowl turned. It started out slow, then the bowl gained speed. Soon, the bowl twirled so fast that it looked blurry.

"What's she doing?" Annie asked softly.

"Maybe she's making a Jane-Be-Gone po-tion," Ben joked, closing the door so Dr. Hauntly couldn't hear them.

Jane curled her fingers into a tight fist and held it in front of Ben's nose. "You bet-ter watch out or you'll be seeing stars! What she needs to make is an antiwerewolf formula."

"Don't start that crazy talk again," Ben said.

Annie opened her mouth to answer him, but she stopped when she heard a strange clicking. It sounded just like giant claws making their way across a wooden floor. And the claws were heading straight for them.

6

Ready or Not

Jane ducked behind Ben. Annie jumped behind Jane. Ben stepped back and tripped over Jane. They all landed in a big pile.

"Why are you sitting on the floor?" Kilmer asked. He smiled down at his three neighbors. Next to Kilmer was his cousin, Fang.

Jane noticed Fang wasn't wearing any shoes. His feet were covered with thick black hair. Each toe ended in a long dirty-looking toenail.

"We're not sitting on the floor," Jane sputtered. "We fell."

Annie untangled herself and stood up. "You scared us," she explained. "We didn't expect to see you here."

Kilmer looked confused. "But I live here," he said.

Annie's face turned red and Jane looked down at her sneakers. Ben didn't bat an eye. "Of course you live here," he said. "Annie means we didn't expect you to find us so soon."

"But I wasn't looking for you," Kilmer said.

"How do you expect to win at hide-and-seek if you don't look for us?" Ben said.

"Hide-and-seek?" Kilmer asked.

"That's right!" Jane yelled. "Hide-and-seek. It's a game. We hide from you and you have to find us. Don't you want to play?"

Fang licked his lips. "How do you play?" he asked.

"It's simple," Annie said. "First, cover your eyes. While you count to one hundred, we hide. Then, you try to find us."

Fang shook his head. "That would be too easy," he said. "I could sniff you out in no time." He sniffed the air to prove his point.

"Besides," Kilmer said, "I want to work on my science project."

Ben rolled his eyes. "We can worry about that the night before it's due," he said.

"Do you mean you haven't even started your project?" Jane asked. "I began my research two weeks ago. It's all about the phases of the moon."

Fang scratched his chin with a long fingernail. "I know a lot about the moon's phases," he said. "I study the moon every night. Maybe I could help you."

"What a great idea!" Kilmer said. "You can bring your project over here and we'll work on them together. Annie can help us, too."

"But Ben hasn't even started his project," Annie argued.

"We can help him think of an idea," Kilmer said.

"All right!" Ben yelled.

Jane didn't cheer. She watched the gray mist oozing from under Dr. Hauntly's laboratory door and whispered, "I have a very bad feeling about this."

7
Animal Control

Annie and Jane hurried down Dedman Street. Jane was carrying her poster about the moon. Annie looked up at Hauntly Manor. "I hope Ben is all right in there." The girls had left Ben at the inn while they went to get Jane's science project.

"Ben is the biggest monster on Dedman Street," Jane told Annie. "A werewolf would get sick just sniffing Ben's socks."

Annie giggled. "They're not white. They're not pink. But phe-ew, they sure do stink!"

Jane nodded. "Even monsters have certain standards!"

"Yeah, they can't stand Ben." Annie giggled. Annie stopped laughing when she saw a truck slowly making its way down Dedman Street. BAILEY CITY ANIMAL CONTROL was painted in big blue letters on the side. The

truck rolled to a stop in front of Hauntly Manor Inn.

Two men hopped out of the truck. One man carried a net. The other one carried a long stick with a rope looped on the end.

"Good afternoon, ladies," one of the men hollered from the road. "We're looking for a wild animal. You haven't seen one around, have you?"

Jane and Annie walked over to the truck. "What kind of wild animal?" Annie asked.

The man carrying the net grinned. "We got a strange report from this neighborhood," he said. "Some kook thinks he heard a wolf last night. Did you happen to see a big hairy wolf?"

"Not exactly," Jane said slowly.

The man with the stick nodded. "We didn't expect to find anything. Whoever heard of a wolf in the middle of Bailey City?" Both men laughed.

While the men laughed, Sparky tore around the corner of Hauntly Manor. Sparky came close to the men, skidded to a stop, and arched her back. She laid her ears flat against her head and hissed. Then she jumped onto the porch and sprang onto a window screen.

"That cat looks like it's being chased by a wolf," the man with the net said.

The other man threw his stick back into the truck. "There's nothing here but a crazy cat," he said. "Let's get out of here."

"Don't worry, girls," the man with the net said. "If we hear any more complaints we'll be back. If there is a wolf, we'll catch it!" The two men from the Bailey City Animal Control Department climbed back into their truck and roared off down Dedman Street.

Annie looked at Jane. Jane looked at Annie. Then they both slowly turned around to look at Hauntly Manor.

8

Spider Names

"We've got to do something," Jane told Annie as they walked up the Hauntlys' front walk. "Those men were talking about a wolf and I know exactly who that wolf is."

The two girls jumped when a growl came from above them. Fang stood on the porch, glaring down at the two girls. He didn't wear a coat, even though it was freezing. Annie noticed that Fang was still barefoot. She stared at his feet and shivered, but it wasn't from the cold. She was sure that Fang's feet were hairier than before.

"Is something wrong?" Fang asked.

"We were just talking about my science project," Jane lied.

Fang smiled. "I've been waiting for you. I

cannot wait to get started. Follow me," he said, disappearing through the door.

Jane and Annie slowly climbed the creaking porch steps of Hauntly Manor. "I don't want to go in there," Annie whispered to Jane. "What if Fang gets us?"

"Werewolves only eat people at night," Jane whispered, "when there's a full moon. We don't have to worry." She held up her poster for Annie to see. "The next full moon isn't until tomorrow night."

"It's about time," Ben said when the girls finally made it to Kilmer's bedroom.

Kilmer's bedroom wasn't like most fourth-graders' rooms. It looked like the darkest night, even though it was bright day outside. That's because the walls and ceiling were painted black. A shiny metal table was pushed up against one wall, and a jumble of big wires trailed down from the ceiling. Kilmer didn't even have a regular bed. Instead, there were black blankets and pillows piled on a wooden slab.

Ben pointed to the metal table. "Wait

until you see Kilmer's project," he told the girls.

Annie and Jane looked at three glass boxes filled with lacy webs. In each box, a giant hairy spider was busy spinning more.

"I'm studying the patterns in webs made by different spiders," Kilmer explained. Jane put her project next to Kilmer's. Then she took three steps back.

"Are you sure they're safe?" Annie asked.

Kilmer looked at the spiders in their glass boxes. "Elvira, Winifred, and Minerva wouldn't hurt anything," he said.

"You named your spiders?" Jane asked.

Kilmer blinked. "Of course," he said. "Doesn't everybody?"

"You've done a lot of work," Ben admitted. "I'll never get my project done."

"You should have started a long time ago," Annie lectured.

"Perhaps you would like to spend the

night," Fang suggested. "Then I could help you. After all, there is plenty of room at the inn."

Annie shivered, Jane gulped, but Ben grinned. "That would be perfect," he said. "I came up with a brilliant idea. I'm going to convince your mother to cook up a science project for me."

Kilmer shook his head. "Do not count on it. My mother's experiments are not always what they seem."

"That would be cheating," Annie said. "You have to do your own project just like Jane and Kilmer."

"I will help you," Fang said.

"We will help each other," Kilmer said. "Let us go ask Father if everyone can stay the night."

As soon as Kilmer and Fang left the room, Jane grabbed Ben's arm. "You're not really spending the night here, are you?" she asked him.

Ben grinned. "Of course I am," he said. "I need Fang's help on my report. The two of you will spend the night, too. Unless you're chicken."

"I'm not scared," Jane said quickly.

"Well," Annie said, "I am. I don't want to stay in this creepy place with a werewolf."

"You can't really believe Fang is a werewolf," Ben said with a laugh.

Annie shrugged. "He does have a lot of hair," she said.

"Teenagers are like that," Ben said. "Just wait until I'm a few years older. I'll have lots of hair, too."

"What about his voice?" Jane argued. "Sometimes it sounds just like a growl."

"It's normal for teenagers' voices to change," Ben said.

"Is it normal for the Bailey City Animal Control to be looking for wolves on Dedman Street?" Jane asked. She told Ben what happened when they left to get her science project.

"Aren't you a little scared?" Annie asked Ben.

"I'm not afraid of Fang," Ben said, "be-

cause he's not a werewolf. He's just a hairy teenager from Transylvania. I'll prove it by sleeping in the same room with him tonight."

"We hope you're right," Annie said. "Because if you're not, you may be sleeping with a werewolf!"

9
Late Night

"I can't believe you talked me into spending the night in a haunted house," Annie complained as the kids came back to the Hauntlys' after eating dinner at their own houses.

"I was hoping my mother would say no," Jane admitted.

Ben lifted the heavy door knocker and shook his head. "You guys are wimps. It'll be exciting. We'll have something to brag about at school."

"I just hope we'll be alive to brag," Annie said right before the huge wooden door creaked open and Kilmer ushered them inside.

The kids stayed up late working on their projects. Kilmer carefully drew pictures of the different webs that Elvira, Winifred, and

Minerva made. Fang helped Annie and Jane make a calendar showing the phases of the moon. Ben sat on the floor and tossed a small rubber ball against the wall.

"I can't think of anything to do," Ben complained.

"You're just scared of hard work," Annie told her brother.

"I'm not scared of anything," Ben snapped.

"Yes, you are," Jane blurted. "You're a big chicken when it comes to working."

Fang tilted his head back and howled with laughter. "Jane just gave me a delicious idea for your project," Fang told Ben.

"What is it?" Ben asked hopefully.

Fang grinned so big his yellow canine teeth showed. "I have some chicken bones that you could put back together to make a chicken skeleton."

"Where did you get those?" Jane asked.

Fang smiled and licked his lips. "Oh, I just collected them. Ben could label the

125

bones and even make a poster showing the parts."

"Will you help me?" Ben asked.

"I'd be happy to help," Fang said. "We'll start now."

Fang hurried from the room, but he soon returned with a glass bowl that reminded Jane of her grandmother's candy dish. Only, Fang's bowl didn't hold chocolates. It was filled with bones. Fang licked his lips when he dumped the bleached bones onto the floor. When he helped Ben sort them, Fang's stomach growled.

Ben and Fang worked very late. Finally, Ben yawned. "I'm so tired, I could sleep in the middle of a bullfight," he said.

Fang didn't look tired at all. He didn't say a word when Ben and Kilmer curled up on the wooden slab and went to sleep.

The girls had already crawled into the strange iron beds in the next room. But no matter how hard they tried, Annie and Jane couldn't sleep. At first, they thought they heard chains rattling in the attic. Then

there was a loud bang as if someone had slammed a door. Outside, the wind whipped through the branches of the dead tree in the Hauntlys' front yard.

Annie pulled a pillow over her head, but that didn't help. The wind blew even harder, and she was sure she heard something besides the wind.

"Ahh-ewwwww."

"Did you hear that?" Annie whispered.

"It's the wind," Jane said, but she didn't sound very sure.

"Ahh-ewwww!"

Annie sat up. "There it is again," she whispered.

Jane nodded. "I hear it, too," she said.

"Ahh-ewww. Ahh-EWWWW. AHH-EWW-WWWW."

Annie grabbed Jane's hand. "Something outside is howling."

"Let's find out what it is," Jane said, jumping out of bed to look out the window. It was nearly midnight, but bright moonlight shone on the Hauntlys' backyard.

"Look," Jane hissed, "on top of that old shed."

Annie gasped. A huge creature was perched on top of the shed. It was definitely bigger than Sparky. It was even bigger than a dog. As the two girls stared, the animal lifted its head to look at the moon and howled a lonely cry.

"We're in big trouble," Annie whimpered. "It's a werewolf and he's howling at the full moon."

"The moon isn't quite full," Jane whispered. "I learned that when it's almost full it's called a gibbous moon. That must be why he is howling. He wants a full moon."

"I have to make sure Ben is okay," Annie said. "And you're coming with me."

The girls pulled their blankets tight around them and crept down the hallway to Kilmer's bedroom. Annie turned the doorknob until the door slowly creaked open. Jane flipped the switch, flooding Kilmer's room with light.

Kilmer and Ben were sleeping on the

wooden slab. When the light came on, Ben sat up and blinked. "What's the big idea?" Ben asked, rubbing his eyes. "You look like two ghosts that got lost in the dark."

Kilmer yawned and shook his head. "No, they don't," he said. "They look nothing like ghosts." He lay back down and went to sleep again.

Annie whispered to Ben. "We heard something," she told Ben. "We were worried about you."

"There's nothing to worry about," Ben told the girls. "We're all sleeping like babies."

"Oh, yeah?" Jane asked. "If that's true, then where is Fang?"

Annie, Jane, and Ben looked around the room. Kilmer was snoring on his slab, but Fang was nowhere to be found.

Just then a dark shadow fell across the room. Slowly, Jane and Annie turned around.

Fang stood in the doorway, and he didn't look happy.

10

Midnight Snacks

The next morning, Hilda Hauntly placed a tray on the big table. Jane, Annie, and Ben stared at the pile of bloody rare meat.

"Mmmm," Fang growled. "My favorite breakfast." He stuck his fork into a big piece of meat still attached to a bone and plopped it on his plate. He picked up the bone and started sucking off the meat.

Ben looked at Fang. "I hope you're not still mad about last night," Ben said. "Remember, you promised to help me finish my project."

Fang stopped gnawing on his bone. "I'm not mad, but you weren't supposed to be out of your room," Fang told Annie and Jane. "I told Aunt Hilda and Uncle Boris I would make sure you went to bed early."

"We're sorry," Annie said with a gulp.

"But," Jane said, looking Fang straight in the eyes, "you weren't in bed, either. Where were you?"

Before he answered, Fang picked at a piece of meat stuck between his front teeth with one of his long fingernails. "I was just having a little midnight snack," he finally said.

"Then you would have heard it, too," Annie said.

"Heard what?" Kilmer asked.

"They thought they heard howling," Ben said with a laugh.

Kilmer and Fang didn't laugh. Instead, they looked down at their breakfast plates.

"You'll still help me finish my project, won't you?" Ben asked Fang again.

Fang nodded. "I'll help," he said.

Boris smiled at Annie, Ben, and Jane. "Aren't you hungry this morning?" he asked. "Perhaps you would prefer eggs."

Ben grinned. "Eggs sound good."

Boris grabbed a tray of yellow blobs and

held it out to Ben. "I make a mean scrambled rat snake egg," he said.

Annie gulped and Jane's face looked as pale as milk.

"Actually," Ben said, "I'm not really that hungry."

"We should get home," Annie added.

"But you haven't eaten," Kilmer said. "A good breakfast is the most important meal of the day."

Annie, Jane, and Ben looked at the gooey rat snake eggs and raw meat. "We'll grab a bite a little later," Annie said. "We should really be going home now. Thanks for letting us spend the night."

"We'll be back later to work on our science projects," Ben said.

"After lunch," Jane added as she took one last look at the bloody meat.

Annie, Jane, and Ben rushed outside. Jane stopped her friends before they went too far. "Now we know for sure," she said. "Fang is one hundred percent werewolf and just two percent teenager."

"You better quit calling my friend names," Ben said.

"Didn't you notice that Fang is the hairiest teenager on the planet?" Jane said. "And he's getting even hairier."

"That would describe any teenager," Ben said. "Fang is really a great guy. Most teenagers wouldn't bother spitting on our shoes. But Fang helped us. I wouldn't even have a science project if it wasn't for him."

Annie nodded. "Ben's right. I like Fang, too. He really is nice and he helped you get the phases of the moon right," she told Jane.

Jane shrugged. "That's because most teenagers aren't werewolves, so they aren't experts on the moon and bones."

"I don't care if Fang is King Kong," Ben said. "He's smart and he helped us with our projects. As far as I'm concerned, Fang can stay here and YOU can fly to Transylvania."

"Even if it means living next door to a hairy werewolf?" Jane asked.

"It doesn't matter what he looks like," Annie told her. "Fang is our friend."

"What about the rest of the neighbors?" Jane asked. "People are complaining about Fang's howling. If he keeps it up, the Animal Control guys will come back. And one of these days, they'll catch Fang."

"Fang is pretty hairy and someone might mistake him for a werewolf when he's kidding around howling," Ben admitted. "We have to help him. I bet Kilmer will help, too."

"I'm sure Kilmer will help us if we ask," Annie said.

"What can we do?" Jane asked.

"We'd better think of something fast," Annie said.

"Don't worry," Ben said. "I have a plan."

11

Werewolf Rescue

"Do you think this will work?" Annie asked.

"Of course," Ben said. It was just starting to get dark and Ben, Annie, and Jane were waiting in front of Hauntly Manor.

Annie shivered in the cold wind. "I hope so," she told Ben.

Jane tossed a snowball in the air. "We're supposed to be pretending to have a snowball fight, remember?"

Annie nodded and reached down to make a snowball. Just then, the back door to Hauntly Manor slammed. Heavy footsteps came straight toward them. Annie was ready to run when a familiar face peeped around the corner of the inn. Kilmer smiled at his three friends. "Are you ready?" Kilmer asked.

"Ready and waiting," Ben said.

"Are you sure Fang is out of sight?" Jane asked.

Kilmer nodded. "He's busy gnawing on a roasted boar's head in the basement," he told them. "I locked the door, just to be sure. Do you really think this will work?"

"It's got to work," Ben said. "Fang's life depends on it."

"Then I better get ready," Kilmer said. He disappeared behind Hauntly Manor just as the huge white Animal Control truck squeaked to a stop in front of the inn. The two men in white jumped out. One man had a net and the other had a gun.

"Oh, my gosh," Annie whispered. "Are they going to kill Fang?"

Jane patted Annie's shoulder. "Don't worry, that's a tranquilizer gun. It just puts animals to sleep."

The man with a net waved at them. "Seems like more of your neighbors heard that animal last night," he said.

"What animal?" Ben asked.

141

The two men shrugged. "Whatever it is, it must be big," the net man said. "The Animal Control office got fifteen calls last night. All around midnight."

"What are you going to do with this animal if you find it?" Ben asked.

The net man shrugged. "Same thing we always do. Put it in a little cage until someone finds a zoo for it."

"Unless it's too wild," the other man said.

"Then what happens?" Annie asked.

The man shrugged. "I'd rather not say. But when a big wild animal gets used to living around humans, they become dangerous. We can't let them wander loose."

"So," the first man asked, "have you kids seen any signs of a wild animal?"

"Well," Ben said. "Maybe back in the toolshed."

The two men ran toward the shed. When they ran into the shed, they got the surprise of their lives. Buckets of dust and cobwebs fell right on their heads. The men were covered with the sticky webs from Elvira, Winifred, and Minerva.

"Help!" the men screamed. "Get us out of this mess."

Annie, Ben, and Jane ran over to the men.

"What is going on here?" one of the men said, wiping dust off his head.

"Nothing but a little kids' stuff," Jane explained. "We're sorry about the mess. But we'll make you a deal. If we promise to make sure the howling stops, will you leave Hauntly Manor alone?"

One of the men shrieked and pulled a big black spider out of his hair. "Listen kid, I never want to see this place again as long as I live. You have a deal." Both men ran out of the backyard, the wheels of their truck screeching as they sped away.

Kilmer came over to his friends after the men had gone. Ben slapped Kilmer on his back. Kilmer reached down and picked up Minerva. "Good girl," Kilmer told the spider.

"Now our only problem is how to keep Fang from howling at the moon," Jane said.

"You do not have to worry about that," Kilmer said. "Fang is going home tomorrow. Right now, I should get Minerva back in her container before she catches cold." Kilmer cuddled his pet spider and walked into Hauntly Manor Inn.

"Whew!" Annie said. "What a night."

"I am going to miss Fang," Ben said. "He's a nice guy."

"A nice werewolf," Jane corrected, "and we're safe from werewolves now that he's leaving."

"You forgot one thing," Ben said. "If Fang can fly out, that means . . ."

"More monsters can fly in," Jane finished.

"What could be weirder than having a werewolf next door?" Annie asked.

Jane shivered. "I don't know, but I have a feeling we're going to find out."

Vampire Trouble

*For Michael and Laura Schafer,
two great neighbors — DD*

*To Myra Finney and Carolyn Floyd —
two friends who appreciate a good story
when they hear one! — MTJ*

1

Batty

"What was that?" Ben yelled. He ducked as a big black thing swooped over his head.

Ben's sister, Annie, shrugged. "It was only a black bird."

"It looked more like a bat to me," Jane said. Jane was in the fourth grade like Ben, and she was Annie's best friend.

Jane threw the football back to Ben as the sinking sun cast long shadows across Ben and Annie's backyard. Jane, Annie, and Ben were teaching their friend Kilmer Hauntly how to play football.

Kilmer was Ben and Annie's next-door neighbor. Kilmer was in the same grade as Ben and Jane, but Kilmer wasn't a normal fourth-grader. He had just moved to Bailey City from Transylvania. Kilmer was very tall and his hair was cut flat across the top

of his head. In fact, Annie thought Kilmer looked just like Frankenstein's monster.

Ben caught Jane's pass and then threw the ball to Kilmer. "Jane, you wouldn't know a bat if it landed on your nose," Ben said.

"Sure I would," Jane said. "I saw a bunch of them when my family went on vacation to Carlsbad Caverns. Hundreds of bats came out of the cave at night. It was creepy."

"It sounds neat to me," Kilmer said. "I would feel right at home."

"Whatever it was," Annie said, pointing to Kilmer's house, "it landed at Hauntly Manor Inn."

Before Kilmer and his family moved in, the house at 13 Dedman Street had been brand-new. Now, paint peeled from the wood and most of the windows were cracked. Every single tree was dead, and scratchy weeds filled the yard. A loose sign swayed in the wind. It said HAUNTLY MANOR INN, but few people ever dared to spend the night there.

Kilmer took one look at the black thing landing on his porch and tossed the football back to Ben. Kilmer threw the ball so hard, Ben fell backward trying to catch it.

"I have to go," Kilmer shouted. "My grandmother is here!" Kilmer stomped out of Ben's yard, his big heavy shoes making footprints in the damp ground.

"I wonder what Kilmer's grandmother is

like," Annie said after Kilmer disappeared inside Hauntly Manor.

Jane shrugged. Then she spoke so softly Ben and Annie had to step closer to hear. "Since Kilmer's mother looks like a mad scientist and his dad is the spitting image of Count Dracula, it's a sure bet," she whispered, "that Kilmer's grandmother is some kind of monster."

Jane had barely said the word "monster" when the door to Hauntly Manor creaked open and heavy footsteps clomped onto the porch. Kilmer waved to his friends. "Come over and meet my grandmother!" he yelled.

"I hope you're wrong about Kilmer's grandmother," Annie said, "or we may be walking into a monster trap!"

2
Grandma Bloodsucker

Kilmer's grandmother stood at the top of the staircase in Hauntly Manor. She wore a long black dress with flowing sleeves that reached all the way to her bright green fingernails. Most of the older women Annie knew had short gray hair, but Kilmer's grandmother had hair as black as a bat's wings and it hung all the way down her back.

"It is so very nice to meet Kilmer's friends," Kilmer's grandmother said slowly as she glided down the steep stairs. "Please, do call me Madame Hauntly." She spoke with the same Transylvanian accent that the rest of the Hauntlys had, and she wore bloodred lipstick.

Annie, Jane, Ben, and Kilmer followed

Madame Hauntly into the living room. The room was painted deep red and filled with dusty antique furniture. Giant spiderwebs stretched across all corners of the large room.

"It's nice to meet you," Annie said politely. Kilmer's grandmother was so tall that Annie had to tilt her head back to see the woman's pale face. "Has it been a long time since you've seen Kilmer?"

Madame Hauntly put a long bony hand on Annie's shoulder and patted it. Annie could feel how cold Madame Hauntly's hand was even through her sweater. "Yes, it has been too long," Madame Hauntly said. "I have missed my Kilmer dearly. My heart has been saddened to be so far from one of my favorite grandsons. Transylvania has been lonely without him."

"And we have missed you," Boris Hauntly said as he came into the room. Kilmer's dad wore a black cape that swirled around his legs as he walked. He set down a huge tray on a dusty table. "I am sure your long flight was tiring, so I prepared some refreshments for you."

Madame Hauntly looked at the tray. Tall glasses were filled with a thick red drink, and a plate held a pile of green blobs floating in grease.

"It looks delicious," Madame Hauntly told her son. She picked up a glass of the red liquid, took a small sip, and smiled. "Perfect," she said. "Warm, just the way I like it."

"How about some green pickled possum toes?" Boris asked the children. He pointed to the green slimy blobs on a cracked china plate.

Ben shook his head. "No, thanks. I had all the possum toes I could eat earlier today."

Annie gulped and quickly stood up. "We'd better go. You'll want to rest after your long flight."

Madame Hauntly stretched her long arms. "I am tired," she said, "but I feel better now that I am here."

Jane inched toward the front door. "It was nice meeting you. I hope you enjoy visiting Bailey City."

Jane, Annie, and Ben hurried out of Hauntly Manor Inn. They stopped on the creaking porch to catch their breath. A loose shutter banged in the wind and Annie jumped when Kilmer's cat, Sparky, ran past her leg. Sparky's fur stood up in all directions as if she had just been shocked.

"It looks like Sparky had some of that gross-looking red goop to drink," Ben said. "That stuff would make anyone's hair stick up."

"Boris' food gave me the creeps," Annie added. "What was that weird stuff Madame Hauntly drank?"

Ben shrugged. "I don't know, but if you want to see something really strange, look over there."

3
Grandma's Bed

A huge truck pulled to a stop in front of Hauntly Manor Inn. Two men dressed in solid black climbed out. They glanced at the three kids, but they didn't smile. Instead, they hurried to the back of the truck and swung open the heavy doors.

"What do you think they're unloading?" Annie asked.

"Probably furniture," Jane said. "My parents' new bed came in that kind of truck."

The men didn't carry a bed out of the truck. Instead, they each held one end of a long, narrow wooden box. The box was made from dark wood, and a lid covered the top. It was so long, a basketball player could stretch out inside and still have room to wiggle his toes. The moving men slowly carried the box up the cracked sidewalk of Hauntly Manor Inn. The kids moved out of the way and watched from Ben and Annie's backyard.

The door to the inn opened and Madame Hauntly glided out onto the sagging porch. "Thank you for bringing my baggage," she said in her thick Transylvanian accent. "I would not be able to sleep a wink without it!"

Jane shook her head. "What would Kilmer's grandmother have in a box like that?"

Annie smiled. "Most grandmothers bring special treats from home when they visit. I bet that box is full of games, toys, and other surprises for the whole family."

Madame Hauntly moved to the front of the porch. But when she stepped into a patch of sun she frowned, and quickly stepped back into the shadows. She spoke in a low voice to the men. "Please," she told them, "carry it to the conservatory." Kilmer's grandmother disappeared into

Hauntly Manor Inn, leading the way for the two moving men and the long wooden box.

Jane, Ben, and Annie knew all about Boris Hauntly's conservatory. It was an entire room full of clay pots and dirt beds where most people would plant flowers, but Boris wasn't like most gardeners. Instead, he filled his beds with special dirt from Transylvania, and the pots contained dead-looking sticks and plants. It looked like a graveyard for petunias.

"Why would Madame Hauntly want the surprises in a room full of dirt?" Ben whispered.

"Maybe the box is full of special dirt for Boris' garden," Annie suggested.

"That's it!" Jane said, snapping her fingers. She grabbed Annie's and Ben's arms and pulled them behind the bushes in their front yard.

"What's wrong with you?" Ben asked. "You act like you saw a swamp monster."

Jane's eyes were wide. "I think I figured

it out. That box is full of special dirt, and it is a surprise for everyone in Bailey City."

"All right!" Ben yelled. "I love surprises."

"Madame Hauntly didn't even meet us until today," Annie said. "Why would she bring us a surprise?"

"This isn't that kind of surprise," Jane told her. "The surprise I'm talking about spells trouble if anyone finds out. Big trouble."

"Madame Hauntly came to visit Kilmer," Annie said. "She didn't come to cause trouble."

"But don't you know what that box is?" Jane asked.

"Sure," Ben said. "It's a trunk, an old-fashioned suitcase."

Annie nodded. "Madame Hauntly is a grandmother. That means she's old. She's probably had that trunk forever."

Jane nodded. "Forever is exactly what I mean. Don't you get it? That box isn't full of dirt for Boris' garden," she explained. "It's full of dirt for herself."

"Why would Madame Hauntly bring dirt all the way from Transylvania?" Ben asked.

"For the same reason Boris and Hilda did when they first moved here," Jane explained. "Everybody knows vampires sleep in coffins. But not everybody knows that vampires can't sleep without soil from their native country."

"What does all of this have to do with our neighbors?" Annie asked.

"Madame Hauntly's box is really her coffin full of dirt from Transylvania," Jane told her. "And those long dirt piles in the conservatory are beds, but they're not for tulips and daffodils. They're for vampires!"

4
Vampire Visitors

"VAMPIRES?" Annie shrieked. "Are you crazy?"

"Shhh," Jane warned. "We don't want Madame Hauntly to hear us."

Jane peeked over the bushes at Hauntly Manor Inn.

"Jane's right," Ben said.

"You mean you agree with Jane?" Annie asked.

Ben grinned. "I agree we don't want Madame Hauntly to hear because she'll think Jane is nuttier than peanut butter."

Jane narrowed her eyes and curled her fingers into a fist. "I'll make you a deal. You take that back," she said, "and I won't give you a black eye."

Before Ben could answer, Annie tugged on his sleeve. Annie's face had suddenly

gone pale, and she looked ready to cry. "Look who's coming!" she said, pointing to the sidewalk.

Mrs. Jeepers was walking slowly down Dedman Street. Mrs. Jeepers was one of the third-grade teachers at Bailey School. Most of the kids said Mrs. Jeepers was a vampire, and Annie believed them. Annie was glad she wasn't in Mrs. Jeepers' class.

Mrs. Jeepers' long red hair was pulled back with a green ribbon, and Annie could see the green brooch Mrs. Jeepers always wore pinned near her throat. Kids in her class said the pin glowed when Mrs. Jeepers rubbed it, and they were sure the brooch was full of magic.

"What is she doing on Dedman Street?" Ben asked. Ben didn't like Mrs. Jeepers very much, either. She had a habit of catching him when he caused trouble, which happened a lot.

"Remember," Annie whimpered, "Mrs. Jeepers is Kilmer's aunt."

Ben, Annie, and Jane watched as Mrs. Jeepers hurried closer. She glanced toward the bush that the three kids had ducked behind. Annie closed her eyes and Jane held her breath. Mrs. Jeepers took a step in their direction, but just then the door to Hauntly Manor Inn squeaked open.

Kilmer jumped onto the porch with his heavy brown shoes and yelled, "Auntie Jeepers, guess who's here?"

Mrs. Jeepers didn't have to guess because Madame Hauntly moved onto the porch and waved.

"Mother!" Mrs. Jeepers yelled. "I am so glad to see you."

"That was a close call," Annie whispered, watching the third-grade teacher rush up the steps to hug Kilmer's grandmother. "I thought we were in big trouble."

"We are," Jane said.

"No, we're not," Ben argued. "Mrs. Jeepers didn't see us."

"It doesn't matter," Jane said. "If

Madame Hauntly is Mrs. Jeepers' mother, that means trouble for us and for everyone here on Dedman Street."

"The only thing this means is that your brain has turned to dust," Ben said.

"Oh, my gosh, everyone says that Mrs. Jeepers is a vampire," Annie said with a gasp. "If that's true, then her mother must be . . ."

"That's right," Jane said. "Madame Hauntly is a vampire and the vampires are taking over Dedman Street!"

5
Spying on a Vampire

"You must have been taking a nap when they handed out brains." Ben poked Jane in the head. "You haven't lost your marbles — you never had any to begin with!"

"I'm smarter than you," Jane said. "I figured out that Kilmer's grandmother is a monster."

Annie gulped. "Maybe we should all go home and put on turtlenecks," she suggested.

Ben pulled his shirt collar down and stretched his neck out. "Here, little vampires, come and get it!" he yelled.

"Shhh," Annie gasped. "Don't do that. What if Madame Hauntly or Mrs. Jeepers hears you?"

"Or Boris Hauntly," Jane added. "If he's

not Count Dracula's twin brother, then I'm
a box of rocks."

"You look like a block of concrete to
me," Ben sneered. "And shame on both
of you for calling Kilmer's poor sweet
grandma a monster."

"I'm sorry," Annie said. "I'm just scared."

"There's nothing to be scared of," Ben
said. "And I'm going to show you."

"What are you going to do?" Jane asked.

"I'm going to keep an eye on Granny and
see what she does," Ben told her. "I'll see

she's just a regular old lady with weird clothes. Unless you're scared, you'll go with me."

"I'll go," Jane said, pulling her collar up, "because I want to watch you get your neck bitten. Then I'll have proof that you're a real monster, too."

Ben didn't say another word. He headed to the back of Hauntly Manor Inn, where the conservatory was located. Ben hid behind a dead elm tree and peered into the big glass room. Jane and Annie came up behind him. "What's going on?" Annie whispered.

"It looks like they're digging," Ben explained. He pointed to the mounds of dirt in the middle of the conservatory.

"Or burying something," Jane said with a gulp. Mrs. Jeepers, Kilmer, Boris Hauntly, and his wife, Hilda, stood beside the mounds. Dead plants surrounded them. Boris and Mrs. Jeepers each had shovels.

Madame Hauntly led the moving men

into the conservatory and pointed to one of the mounds. The men gently set the huge box down and hurried out of the room.

As soon as the men left, Madame Hauntly got on her knees beside the box and kneeled down. She pressed her lips to the dirt.

"Yuck!" Annie said. "She's kissing dirt."

"Maybe she's eating it," Ben said. "It has to taste better than green pickled possum toes."

"Where's she going?" Annie asked. The three kids watched Madame Hauntly leave the room.

"She's probably going to turn into a bat and fly to the nearest cave," Jane said.

"If she's looking for an empty cave, your head would be perfect," Ben joked.

"Ha-ha." Jane pretended to laugh. "I'll make you a deal. You go jump in the nearest lake and I'll throw you a life preserver . . . a concrete one."

Ben stuck out his tongue at Jane and Jane pushed Ben. Annie was the only one who saw the dark figure approaching them, and Annie didn't notice until it was too late.

6
Dead Darlings

"My darling children," Madame Hauntly said, grabbing Ben and Jane by the shoulders. "I am so glad to see you again. I noticed you watching through the window. Please join us in the conservatory for the festivities."

Ben shook his head quickly. "No, thanks," he said. "We were just leaving."

"Oh, but I insist," Madame Hauntly said, pulling Ben and Jane toward the back of the house.

"Help," Ben squeaked at Annie. "Save me."

Madame Hauntly chuckled. "You Americans are so funny. I love your humor."

"I love living," Ben said. Annie shrugged and followed Ben, Jane, and Madame Hauntly into the darkened conservatory.

Blinds had been lowered throughout the glass room, and hundreds of candles sat in the dirt, casting shadows on Madame Hauntly's face.

"Please be seated," Madame Hauntly said. "We will begin." Ben, Annie, and Jane sat on one of the dirt mounds.

"What are they beginning?" Annie whispered.

"They're going to make us into dead darlings," Ben explained.

Jane punched Ben in the shoulder. "I thought you didn't believe that Madame Hauntly is a vampire."

Ben shrugged. "I don't know what to think."

Kilmer, Boris, Hilda, Mrs. Jeepers, and Madame Hauntly seated themselves on the dirt mounds around the children. "How should we start?" Madame Hauntly asked.

"Tell the one about Great-grandfather Hauntly," Kilmer said.

Madame Hauntly nodded. "Many, many years ago there lived a boy named Edwardo

Hauntly. He grew up strong and handsome, with flaming red hair." Madame Hauntly paused and smiled at Mrs. Jeepers.

"Edwardo learned to be a farmer, a good farmer. He had a beautiful wife and six children. But an evil man lived nearby who called himself Vlad. This evil man tried to steal Edwardo's land and even Edwardo's wife. For a time, Vlad partly succeeded. Edwardo's wife talked Edwardo into leaving the land, but without the land to provide their food, the family soon became hungry. Edwardo sneaked away to fight Vlad.

"The battle went on for six days. Vlad was a fierce fighter, but Edwardo fought for his six children and his wife. Every time Edwardo was near losing, he thought of his hungry children and he fought harder. Finally, on the sixth day, Edwardo won the battle and Vlad agreed to give back Edwardo's land, but only on one condition."

"What condition?" Ben asked.

Madame Hauntly smiled, showing her huge eyeteeth. "Edwardo agreed to only

EDWARDO

farm at night and never appear on his land during the day. Even now, Hauntlys shun the daylight as often as possible, staying in the dark as a tribute to Edwardo and his bravery."

"That's some story," Annie said.

"Tell another one," Kilmer asked his grandmother.

"Is that what you're doing here?" Ben asked. "Telling stories?"

Hilda Hauntly nodded, her wild hair bobbing up and down. "Certainly, what did you think we were going to do?"

Ben gulped. "Oh, nothing."

"Would you like to share a story?" Madame Hauntly asked. "I am sure such nice young people have wonderful stories to share."

Annie smiled, but shook her head. "We'd love to hear more of your stories."

Madame Hauntly patted Annie on the head and started another story.

Annie, Ben, and Jane sat spellbound as Madame Hauntly told tales of long-ago times and ancient relatives. Every story held excitement, adventure, and danger. They were exactly the type of stories Ben loved.

Finally, Madame Hauntly held up her

hand. "Enough stories," she said. "It is time for an old woman to rest."

"No," Ben begged. "Don't quit."

Madame Hauntly smiled and laid down on top of one of the big piles of dirt. She closed her eyes, folded her hands on her chest, and two minutes later she was snoring.

"We'd better leave her alone," Kilmer told the kids. "Grandmother likes to nap during the day. She has more energy when it's dark outside."

Annie shivered when she saw Madame Hauntly's still form. "Thanks for the stories," she said quickly. "We'll leave now."

"Did you see her sleeping in the dirt?" Jane asked later as the kids walked home. "I told you she was a vampire."

"She's a cool lady," Ben said. "I wouldn't care if she were Queen Vampirola."

Annie nodded. "She did tell neat stories. I wish our grandmother would visit and tell fun stories like that. I guess Madame

Hauntly was exhausted after traveling all the way from Transylvania."

"That's because she flew with her own wings," Jane said. "I think Madame Hauntly was that big bat we saw."

"Put a sock in it," Ben said. "I plan to have fun with Madame Hauntly and listen to all her stories. Kilmer said we can go with him tomorrow when he shows his grandmother around Bailey City."

"And if his grandmother bites us on the neck," Jane said, "we can all fly around Bailey City together as bats!"

7

Delicious Treats

The next day, Kilmer and his grandmother weren't ready until the sun sank
low in the evening sky. Ben, Jane, and Annie
climbed the steps to Hauntly Manor. They
took a step back when the door slowly
swung open and Madame Hauntly glided
out onto the porch. She wore a long black
dress that dragged on the ground, and her
lips were covered with deep red lipstick.

"I am looking forward to seeing all the
delicious treats Bailey City has to offer,"
Madame Hauntly told the children.

"We should show your grandmother the
playground," Ben said.

"Why would a grandmother want to see
the playground?" Annie asked.

But Madame Hauntly clapped her hands.
"I would enjoy meeting more of your

friends," she told Kilmer. "The playground is the perfect place."

Kilmer and Madame Hauntly headed down Dedman Street. Madame Hauntly's dress was so long, the kids couldn't see her feet. They could hear Kilmer's heavy shoes hitting the sidewalk, but Madame Hauntly didn't make a sound.

Ben hurried after Kilmer and his grandmother. Annie and Jane followed close behind. They didn't slow down until they reached the Bailey School playground.

Several kids were kicking a soccer ball. A boy named Huey grabbed the soccer ball and ran over to Kilmer. "How about a game of soccer?" he asked.

A girl named Carey nodded. "We need more kids to make a team," she said. Then Carey held out her hand to Madame Hauntly. "My name is Carey," she said. "It's nice to meet you."

When Madame Hauntly licked her lips and smiled, Carey dropped her hand to her side and took a giant step back.

"We can't play," Kilmer explained. "I am showing my grandmother around Bailey City."

"Of course you can play," Madame Hauntly said. "I will rest under the branches of this beautiful oak tree."

Jane pointed to the sky. "The sun is ready to set. There are only a few minutes of light left. We won't be playing long."

The group of kids raced across the playground after the soccer ball, leaving Madame Hauntly in the shadows of the oak tree.

When Kilmer kicked the ball, Madame Hauntly cheered. She yelled for Ben, Jane, and Annie, too.

Finally, Annie told Kilmer, "We'd better go back to your grandmother."

But when the kids looked toward the shadows of the oak tree, Madame Hauntly was nowhere to be seen.

8

Monster Shakes

"Where did she go?" Carey asked.

"She disappeared into thin air!" Annie shrieked.

Kilmer didn't seem worried. He held his hands to his mouth and hollered, "Grandmother? Where did you fly off to?"

High in the oak tree, leaves rustled when Madame Hauntly pulled back a few branches to wave. "I am perched up here," she called down. "It was the perfect place to watch your game."

"Cool," Ben said. "A grandmother that climbs trees!" All the kids raced to the tree to see if Madame Hauntly needed help climbing back down. But by the time they reached the tree, she was already standing on the ground.

"What treat will you show me next?" Madame Hauntly asked.

"Burger Doodle!" Ben yelled. "They have the best Doodlegum Shakes in town!"

Madame Hauntly licked her lips so they glistened. "I would enjoy sipping a drink," she said. "I will buy everyone a shake!"

"We'll have to hurry," Jane said. "It's getting dark."

Madame Hauntly glanced at the darkening sky. The moon was already low on the horizon. "There is nothing to fear from darkness," she told the children. "I have told your parents we may be late. So let us enjoy the night!"

Madame Hauntly glided down the sidewalk with Kilmer leading the way. Before Annie, Jane, and Ben could join them, Carey reached out and grabbed them. "How did she do that?" Carey whispered. "Nobody has climbed that high in the oak tree before."

Annie shrugged. "She probably has one

of those stair climbers at home. My mother has one, but she never uses it."

Carey shook her head so hard, her blond curls bounced. "There is no way she could climb that fast."

"But she had to climb up there," Jane said. "That's the only way to get up in a tree."

"There is another way," Carey said slowly.

"How?" Annie asked.

Carey looked each of them in the eyes before answering. "By flying!"

Annie giggled and Ben laughed out loud. But Jane didn't say a word.

"You have to admit," Carey added, "there is something strange about Kilmer's grandmother."

"Don't be silly," Ben said. "Kilmer's grandmother is the coolest adult I've ever met. She knows how to have fun with kids. She's even going to treat us to Doodlegum Shakes."

"Either that," Carey said slowly, "or she's fattening us up."

"For what?" Annie asked.

"For dinner!" Carey told them. "I think Kilmer's grandmother is a vampire and we're her next meal. I bet instead of going to drive-through windows she goes to fly-throughs!"

Ben laughed so hard, Kilmer heard him and stopped.

"Is there something the matter?" Madame Hauntly called to them.

Carey grabbed Ben's elbow. "Don't go with her," she said. "It may be the last thing you do."

Ben glared at Carey's hand holding his arm. "If you don't let go of me, it WILL be the last thing you do," he told her, shaking his arm free from her grasp. "Besides, you're batty. The only weird thing about Madame Hauntly is that she's being nice to you." With that, Ben ran to catch up with Kilmer and his grandmother.

"We'll see," Carey said as she followed behind Jane and Annie.

Burger Doodle was deserted except for the kids and Madame Hauntly. They all ordered milk shakes and sat in a dark corner. Madame Hauntly closed her eyes and sucked her strawberry shake with loud slurping noises.

Carey pushed her shake away and stared at Kilmer's grandmother before standing up and brushing her blond curls back from her face. "That is the most disgusting thing I ever heard," she said out loud.

Jane and Annie gasped when Madame Hauntly slowly opened her eyes and stared straight at Carey.

Ben just grinned. "Then you haven't heard the noises I can make," he said with a laugh. "I know how to make sounds that would make you want to crawl in a cave and not come out for ten years," he told Carey. "Do you want me to prove it?"

Carey glared at Ben. "You are as strange as Kilmer and his grandmother," she said. "I can't decide who is the worst. You're all monsters, and I plan to do something about it!"

9
Carey Strikes Again

After Carey stormed out of Burger Doodle, Jane leaned over to Madame Hauntly.

"We're sorry," Jane said to Madame
Hauntly.

"Carey can be very rude," Annie added.

Madame Hauntly smiled at Kilmer and
his friends. "I have learned not to fear what
people say," she told them. "They cannot
hurt me with their words."

Ben shrugged. "She's gone now. She
won't bother us anymore." But Ben was
wrong. He forgot one thing. Carey could be
very stubborn.

The next morning, Carey marched down
Dedman Street. She stopped right in front
of Hauntly Manor Inn and jabbed a big sign
into the ground.

Ben and Annie watched from the window of their house. "What is she doing?" Annie asked.

Ben headed for the door. "There's only one way to find out."

Jane was already standing in Ben and Annie's front yard. Ben and Annie hurried to join her so they could see Carey's sign. In big black letters Carey had written BEWARE OF VAMPIRES. A picture of fangs dripping blood was drawn below the words.

"Is she crazy?" Ben asked. "She can't just go sticking signs in people's yards."

"Carey is used to doing whatever she wants to," Annie said.

"That's true," Jane said. Carey's dad was the president of Bailey City Bank, and Jane never liked the way Carey always got her way.

"We can't let the Hauntlys see the sign," Annie said. "It will hurt their feelings."

Ben checked his watch. "We don't have to worry about Kilmer's folks. They never come outside much during the day. We'll just wait until Carey goes away, and then we'll take down her sign," he said.

Ben was right. Kilmer's parents didn't come outside, but Kilmer did. "What is going on?" he asked Ben.

Ben shrugged. "Carey is just being a wet turnip."

"I'm sorry," Annie said. "I hope she didn't hurt your feelings."

Kilmer shook his head. "Remember, my grandmother said to not let what people say hurt you."

"Don't worry about it," Ben said as Kilmer headed back to Hauntly Manor. "I'm sure she'll go home soon."

But Carey didn't go away. Instead, she put something around her neck. Then she picked up another sign and started marching up the sidewalk, straight toward Ben, Jane, and Annie. With each step she chanted three words. "GO HOME, VAMPIRES!"

Carey stomped right past Ben, Annie, and Jane. When she did, the three kids nearly choked.

"What is that smell?" Annie asked, holding her nose.

"I always knew girls were stinky," Ben said. "But this is worse than a sewer!"

Jane ignored Ben and pointed to Carey. "That smell isn't Carey," she explained. "It's her necklace."

"What is it made from?" Ben asked. "Wet dog fur?"

"No," Jane said. "It's made from garlic to keep away vampires."

The three kids watched Carey go all the way down to the corner of Dedman Street. Then she turned around and headed back. By the time she was halfway down the street, three other neighbors had come outside to watch.

"This has gone too far," Ben said, stomping his foot. "The rest of the neighborhood is starting to notice. We have to stop her."

"What if everybody in the neighborhood joins in with Carey?" Jane asked.

"That's exactly why we should stop her," Annie said. "Carey is being rude to the Hauntlys."

"This is our chance to make sure Carey doesn't get her way for once," Ben added.

"We've got to do something," Annie said. "After all, Kilmer's grandmother did treat us to Doodlegum Shakes."

"And she tells great stories," Ben said.

"She's the nicest adult on Dedman Street," Annie said.

"All right," Jane said. "How can we stop Carey?"

Ben grinned. "I'm glad you asked," he said. "I have the perfect plan!"

10
Plan V

Carey marched up and down Dedman Street until the sun climbed high in the sky. Then her mother called her home for lunch. Before leaving, Carey yelled, "I'll be back first thing tomorrow."

"She's finally gone home," Ben told Jane and Annie. "It's time to put Plan V into action."

"What is Plan V?" Annie asked.

Ben smiled. "Plan Vampire, just like we talked about. As in, save our friendly neighborhood vampires from the real bloodsucker named Carey."

"I hope this isn't being too mean," Annie said when Ben stopped talking.

Jane shook her head. "Carey deserves to be put in her place for once. She's always acting like she's better than everyone else.

209

She didn't have to be so rude to Madame Hauntly."

"Maybe this will teach her a lesson," Ben said. "Besides, if we don't do something, she's not going to let poor Madame Hauntly alone."

"All right," Annie said. "Let's do it. Commence Plan V." Annie took a jar of green goop, a bag of funny pajamas that her aunt May had given her for a joke, and a box of hair rollers that she'd borrowed from her mother. She headed over to Carey's house.

"Hi, Carey!" Annie said with a smile. "Can you play?"

Carey didn't get a lot of people coming over to her house, so Annie was invited in right away. Annie played for quite a while, and when she left she was empty-handed.

"I feel very guilty," Annie said when she got home. "Carey really needs a friend."

"If she wasn't so mean, she'd have lots of friends," Ben pointed out.

Jane patted Annie's shoulder. "You can be her friend tomorrow, after Plan V works."

"All right," Annie said with a sigh. "I told her to be ready at seven tonight. She said she was looking forward to a total beauty makeover."

Ben nodded, then threw on his vampire cape, while Annie and Jane painted their faces white and drew on bloody fangs.

Next, Jane made phone call after phone call and tried to talk in a very grown-up voice. "Yes." She nodded after talking for a while. "It will be a very newsworthy event."

211

11

Meanest Monster of All

As the sun faded from the sky, the three kids emerged from Ben's house looking like a kid's worst nightmare.

First, the kids pulled up the BEWARE OF VAMPIRES sign from the ground at Hauntly Manor Inn. They walked down the block to Olympus Lane and sank the sign into the ground in front of a huge white mansion. Annie giggled. "I hope Carey likes her new lawn ornament." The kids didn't have to wait long to find out, because Carey flew out of the house in a rage.

"What are you doing?" Carey yelled.

Annie and Jane shouted, "Go home, vampires! Go home, vampires!"

Ben couldn't shout. After looking at Carey, he couldn't do anything but laugh.

Ben bent over laughing and pointed at Carey.

Carey did make a funny picture with her face covered in green goop. Her hair was in bright green and pink hair rollers. She wore pajamas with feet in them that made her look like a big rabbit. The pajamas even had a carrot dangling on the side.

Before Carey could yell again, the real excitement began. A television van pulled up and a reporter from WMTJ hopped out. A cameraman pointed his camera right at Carey and the kids. Lots of people came out of their houses to see what was going on. Even the Hauntlys came up behind Ben.

"We've heard a rumor of monsters being seen in the neighborhood," the reporter said, sticking a microphone in Ben's face. "Do you have any comment?" he asked.

Ben smiled and grabbed the micro-phone.

"Oh, no," Jane moaned. "Here goes the biggest show-off in the history of Bailey City."

"Yes," Ben said, ignoring Jane. "It's true. There really is a monster in the neighborhood."

Annie held her breath and looked at Madame Hauntly.

"And right now," Ben continued, "I would like to introduce you to the biggest monster ever."

Carey glared at Madame Hauntly. But Ben didn't shove the microphone in front of Madame Hauntly, he held it in front of Carey. "I'd like all of Bailey City to meet the meanest monster of all — Carey in her pj's!"

"Awww!" Carey screamed and put her hands in front of her face. She turned and ran back into her big white house, with the little bunny tail flapping behind her.

Kilmer and Madame Hauntly laughed. "Ben," Madame Hauntly said, "you are a wonderful young man to stand up for an old bat like me."

Ben shrugged. "People on Dedman Street have to stick up for one another."

Madame Hauntly patted Ben on the shoulder. "You have made me feel so welcome," she said. "Perhaps I should consider making Dedman Street my permanent home."

"That would be neat," Ben said. "Then I could brag to all my friends about the cool grandma I have next door to me."

Madame Hauntly smiled, showing her pointy eyeteeth before floating off toward

Hauntly Manor Inn along with the rest of the Hauntlys.

"Did she say she might stay here?" Jane asked.

Annie smacked herself in the head. "Oh, no," she said. "What have we done? Dedman Street is getting a little too full of monsters."

Ben shrugged again and smiled. "Look at it this way. As long as they're on our side, we have nothing to worry about."

Kilmer's Pet Monster

*To Barbara and Lee Beckham and their
pet monster, Pistol Pete.—MTJ*

For Kevin Gibson, a great nephew—DD

1

Hocus Pocus Visitor

"What took you so long?" Jane asked Ben and Annie. "We're going to be late for school." Jane had been waiting for Annie and her older brother, Ben, in front of their house for at least ten minutes. They always walked to school together.

Annie pointed to Ben. "Ben couldn't find his math book."

Ben started to argue but Jane stepped between them. "We don't have time for a fight," she said as she led them to the house next door. "Let's get Kilmer."

It wasn't too long ago that the house at 13 Dedman Street was brand-new. Then the Hauntlys moved in. Now the paint was cracked and the lawn was crispy brown. All the trees in the yard were dead sticks, and the inn's shutters hung at crazy angles. A lopsided sign that said HAUNTLY MANOR INN creaked in the morning breeze.

"This place looks worse every day," Annie said.

Ben shrugged. "I think it's cool."

"It doesn't matter how it looks," Jane reminded them. "But it does matter if we're late for school."

The three friends made their way up the cracked sidewalk. Just as they started climbing the steps, a stranger stepped out from the shadows of the porch. The three kids took a giant step back and looked up into the wrinkled face of the strange lady.

She wore a long black robe and pointy black shoes. Except for silver streaks, even her long frizzy hair was black. She held a broom, but she didn't look as if she planned to sweep any of the cobwebs hanging from the railing. Instead, she propped the broom against the house and smiled, showing crooked yellow teeth.

"Good morning, my little ones," the stranger said.

Ben stared and Annie gulped, but Jane held out her hand. "You must be the Hauntlys' newest guest," she said. "My name is Jane. Did you just get here?"

When the old woman shook Jane's hand, Annie noticed the old woman's nails were painted a sickly shade of green. "I flew in last night," the stranger said, "by the light of the moon. I am Priscilla Pocus."

"My name is Annie and this is my brother, Ben," Annie said politely. "We live next door. Welcome to Bailey City."

Just then Sparky leaped onto the porch railing. Sparky was Kilmer's pet cat, but she was anything but tame. The kids were used to the way Sparky hissed and darted around Hauntly Manor as if ghosts had her by the tail.

"The first thing you should know," Ben warned Priscilla, "is not to pet that cat. She has long claws and she's not afraid to use them."

Priscilla's laugh gave Annie a serious case of goose bumps. "Sparky doesn't

224

scare me," Priscilla said. *"Feline claws, whiskers, and fur. I'll scratch your chin and hear you purr."*

The old lady finished her rhyme then reached out a single green fingernail to scratch Sparky's chin. The kids could hear Sparky's rumbling purr all the way across the porch.

"Wow," Ben said. "I've never seen Sparky let anyone except Kilmer get close to her."

"I didn't think Sparky knew how to purr," Jane added.

Priscilla laughed again. Annie noticed that the old lady's laugh sounded like paper being crumpled. "I have a way with cats," Priscilla said.

"I wish we could stay to talk more," Jane said. "But we're late for school. We came to get Kilmer."

"I will get him for you," Priscilla said. Sparky hopped off the railing and rubbed against the stranger's leg. Priscilla pointed to an old rocking chair and looked at Sparky. *"Hop in that chair. I won't be long, wait for me there."* The words were barely out of her mouth when Sparky jumped in the chair and curled into a little ball. Then Priscilla Pocus disappeared inside Hauntly Manor Inn.

"I can't believe it," Ben said. "That cat is acting so friendly."

"I wouldn't get too close to Sparky," Jane warned. "She may like Priscilla, but she still thinks we're walking, talking scratching posts."

"It's strange seeing Sparky act calm," Ben said.

"Sparky's not the strangest thing we've seen this morning," Annie said.

"Everything is strange about Hauntly Manor Inn," Jane said with a laugh.

Annie nodded. "But I think things just got a little stranger," she said, "when Priscilla Pocus flew into town."

Annie couldn't say any more because just then the door to Hauntly Manor Inn slowly creaked open.

2

Pet Show

Kilmer stepped onto the porch. Kilmer was in the fourth grade with Jane and Ben, but he was at least a foot taller. With his heavy brown shoes and flattop haircut, Annie thought their friend looked just like Frankenstein's monster, especially today because his shirt was torn in three places.

"What happened to you?" Ben asked. "It looks like a tiger played tug-of-war with your shirt."

Kilmer glanced down at his shirt. "I was playing with Bruno," he said. "It was so much fun, I forgot about the time."

"Who is Bruno?" Annie asked.

"Priscilla's pet," Kilmer told her. "He likes it in our basement because it reminds him of the cave where he usually lives."

"What kind of pet lives in a cave?" Ben asked.

"You can tell us about Bruno later," Jane interrupted. "We have to hurry or we'll be late for school."

The four kids raced down Dedman Street toward Bailey Elementary School. "I think we made it on time," Annie said. "There's still a bunch of kids on the playground." She pointed to a crowd of third-graders gathered under a giant oak tree.

"I wonder what they're doing," Jane said.

"There's only one way to find out," Ben told them. He raced toward the oak tree. Annie, Jane, and Kilmer ran after him.

A boy named Howie stood in the middle of the crowd of kids. He held a purple piece of paper. "When is it?" a girl named Liza asked him.

Howie looked at the paper and read, "The Bailey City Pet Contest will be held this Saturday in Bailey City Park. A brand-new bicycle will be awarded to the owners of the most unusual and talented pet."

"All right!" a boy named Eddie yelled. "I'm entering my aunt's dog. Diamond is sure to win a pet contest."

Carey lived near Ben, Annie, Jane, and Kilmer. She stepped in front of Eddie and shook her head so hard her blond curls bounced. "My poodle is better than your aunt's Dalmatian," she said.

"My parrot is more talented than both of your stupid dogs," a girl named Issy bragged. "I'll win that bicycle."

"Are there any rules?" a third-grader named Melody asked before a fight broke out.

Howie nodded. "All pets must be well-trained and able to get along with other pets. They must be on a leash or in a cage."

The kids all started talking at once. Everyone was planning on entering their pets.

Ben, Annie, Kilmer, and Jane walked toward the school door. "I sure would like to have a new bicycle," Ben said. "Mine is all banged up."

"At least you have one," Annie pointed out. "Kilmer doesn't have a bike."

"He could enter his cat," Jane said with a giggle. "Maybe Sparky wouldn't bite off the judge's hand."

Ben shook his head. "Howie's paper said the prize would be given to an unusual pet. I think Kilmer should enter Minerva, Winifred, and Elvira." The kids knew all about Kilmer's three pet spiders. Kilmer had studied the patterns of their webs for the fourth-grade science fair. "I'm going to

talk Mom into letting me get a big iguana so I can enter the contest, too," Ben added.

"Don't bother," Jane said with a laugh. "I plan on winning that contest."

"How?" Annie said. "You don't have a pet."

"Easy," Jane told them. "I'll put a leash around Ben's neck and tell everyone he's my pet ape."

"That won't work," Annie said. "He isn't smart enough to learn any tricks."

"Very funny, monkey breath," Ben said.

"Wait!" Kilmer yelled, interrupting his friends. "I have a better idea."

"What could be better than creepy-crawly spiders?" Ben asked.

Kilmer smiled. "Priscilla's pet," he told them. "Bruno is most unusual. Bailey City has never seen anything like him."

Annie pulled on Jane's sleeve. "What kind of pet would Priscilla have?" Annie whispered.

"If Kilmer thinks it's unusual, then it can only be one thing," Jane said slowly. "A pet monster."

3
Pet Spies

By Friday afternoon, every kid at Bailey Elementary was busy getting ready for the pet show. Ben, Annie, Jane, and Kilmer stood on the playground and watched Eddie with his aunt's dog. He was trying to get the Dalmatian to walk, sit, and heel, but Prince Diamond was too busy chasing squirrels and dragging Eddie along behind him.

Carey laughed and reached down to straighten the bow on her poodle's head. Then Carey and her poodle pranced by Ben, Annie, Jane, and Kilmer.

"It's no fair," Ben complained. "Mom won't let me get an iguana. Everybody else has a cool pet except me."

Annie tapped her brother on the shoulder. "I don't have a pet."

"Me, neither," Jane added.

"You two don't count," Ben grumbled.

"Why can't you get a lizard?" Kilmer asked.

"Mom said they're too creepy," Ben said.

Kilmer looked confused. "But lizards are cuddly," he argued.

"Not according to my mom," Annie said.

"I'll be the only kid that doesn't have a chance to win that new bike," Ben grumbled.

"You could borrow Minerva, Winifred, and Elvira," Kilmer said.

Ben slapped Kilmer on the back. "Do you mean it?" Ben asked. "You'd really let me borrow your spiders?"

"Of course," Kilmer said. "They like you. I'm sure they wouldn't mind."

"Then we have to hurry home," Ben said. "I have lots of work to do."

The four kids ran toward Dedman Street. On the way, they passed Issy's house. Issy sat on her porch, a parrot perched on her shoulder.

"Hey!" Issy called. "Don't you want to stop and see what my parrot can do? I've been training Filbert for the pet show."

Ben would have kept running except Annie reached out and grabbed his elbow. "Be nice," she whispered. "Issy doesn't have many friends."

Ben shrugged. "That's because nobody likes her," he said matter-of-factly.

"We should see what she's training her pet to do," Jane pointed out.

"Are you talking about spying?" Ben asked.

Jane nodded. "It might help you win the contest."

Ben grinned. "Why didn't you say so in the first place? Let's go do some pet spying."

The four friends walked up the sidewalk and stopped in front of Issy. Isabel Hart was in the fourth grade with Ben, Kilmer, and Jane, but she thought she was the prettiest girl in all of Bailey City. Ben tried to stay as far away from her as possible.

238

"We'd love to see what your bird can do," Jane said.

The parrot's bright green wings fluttered. "Filbert want a cracker?" Issy asked the bird.

Filbert looked at Issy. He cocked his head to one side and said, "Awk!"

"Is that it?" Ben blurted. "You trained your bird to say awk?"

Issy huffed. "I just started. By tomorrow he'll be talking up a storm," she told them. "I'll win that bicycle and you won't win a thing."

"And the sky will turn purple," Ben said with a laugh.

"You're just jealous," Issy told Ben, "because you don't have a pet to enter in the contest."

Ben stood up tall. "I do too. And so does Kilmer. Our pets are much better than yours."

"What are they?" Issy asked, a worried look on her face.

Kilmer spoke before Ben had a chance. "It's a surprise," he said.

Ben nodded. "You won't find out until tomorrow," he told her.

But as the four friends walked away from Issy's house, Ben grabbed Kilmer's arm. "If Issy really gets her featherbrained bird to talk, we'll be in trouble," he said. "We have to train our pets to do something special, just in case."

Kilmer nodded. "That won't be a problem. Bruno is very talented. He can do things no other pet can do."

"Are you sure?" Jane asked. "After all, we haven't even seen him."

Kilmer scratched his head and sighed. "Bruno is a bit shy," Kilmer said. "He's not used to being around people."

"Are you sure he's safe?" Annie asked.

Kilmer thought for a moment. "It will be safe," he finally said.

"I hope you're right," Jane said, "or the people of Bailey City may be in for the surprise of their lives!"

4
Hauntly Pet Tricks

Kilmer's parents sat on the porch when the kids reached Hauntly Manor Inn. Kilmer's father, Boris Hauntly, smiled, showing his pointy eyeteeth. Boris was very tall and always wore a black cape. If it wasn't for his red hair, Boris would be a dead ringer for Dracula. "Would you like to come in for an after-school treat?" Boris asked.

Kilmer's mother, Hilda Hauntly, smiled. "We just finished baking some delicious peanut butter and worm cookies." Hilda was a scientist and stirred up unusual inventions, but her cooking inventions were the strangest of all. Jane, Ben, and Annie were never brave enough to try any of the Hauntlys' recipes.

"No thank you," Ben said. "I have to get

ready for the pet show. Kilmer is letting me borrow his spiders."

"And we're going to help him," Jane said quickly.

Kilmer nodded. "Bruno must know how to do tricks if I am to win."

Boris smiled. "Teaching Bruno tricks sounds like fun. Perhaps you can teach him to swoop down and grab furry creatures in his claws."

Hilda nodded. "Or Bruno could learn how to open his jaws wide so the judge can stick his head inside."

"But what if he makes a mistake and closes his mouth?" Annie asked.

"Hmmm, that could be a little messy," Hilda agreed. "Will there be any spare judges on hand?"

"I'm not sure," Annie said. "Maybe Kilmer should try teaching Bruno something else."

"Before I do anything," Kilmer interrupted, "I have to get Bruno to stay on a leash."

Boris' eyes opened wide. "I don't think Bruno has ever been on a leash before," he said. "Are you sure it can be done?"

"He has to be on a leash," Ben told Boris. "It's one of the rules."

Hilda stood up. "Perhaps we should help," she said. "After all, Bruno isn't used to cooperating."

Boris nodded. "We will meet you in the basement," he told Kilmer. "Perhaps the three of us can tame Bruno." Hilda and Boris opened the door and entered the darkness of Hauntly Manor Inn.

"Bruno sounds big," Annie said.

"And mean," Jane added.

Kilmer shrugged. "He's not so bad once he gets to know you."

"I think I'll stick to spiders," Ben said. "I'll try training them while you work with Bruno."

Kilmer nodded. "I'll get them for you." Kilmer left Ben, Annie, and Jane alone on the porch.

"I hope Kilmer knows what he's doing," Annie said.

Jane nodded. "If Bruno is half the monster I think he is," she said slowly, "we may be in big trouble!"

5
Spider Tricks

"What are you doing?" Jane asked Ben. Jane and Annie were sitting on the Hauntlys' porch steps, waiting for Kilmer, while Ben was doing a headstand on the grass.

"I'm trying to teach these spiders some tricks," Ben explained.

Annie giggled. "I don't think spiders can learn to stand on their heads," she said.

"Sure they can," Ben told her. "You two stand on your heads and help me."

"Not in your lifetime," Jane said and scooted farther away from the three glass spider cases. She moved back toward the window and startled Sparky. Sparky was stretched out on the windowsill and did not look pleased at being disturbed.

"Maybe you could teach them another

trick," Annie suggested. "Like diving into a glass of water."

"Do spiders like water?" Jane asked.

"Who cares?" Ben asked, grabbing Sparky's water dish and sliding it into Minerva's case. "It would be a neat trick."

Jane watched Minerva scamper away from the black bowl. "Minerva doesn't seem too interested," Jane said.

"It's not fair," Ben complained. "If Mom had let me get an iguana I wouldn't have this problem."

"I know," Jane said, giggling. "Why don't you climb to the top of the roof and jump headfirst into the little water bowl yourself? Maybe Minerva just needs to see you do it."

"Very funny," Ben said with a sneer. "I hope Minerva has babies and they all come to live in your underwear."

"Don't get mad," Annie told her brother. "Maybe you just need to keep trying."

"I could try until my teeth rot," Ben

grumbled. "These spiders don't want to do anything exciting."

HISSSSSS! GRRRRRR! RRROAAARRR!

"I don't think Minerva made that noise," Annie said with a gulp.

"It wasn't me," Ben said.

Jane looked toward the Hauntlys' basement window. "It sounded to me like it came from the basement."

HISSSSSS! GRRRRRRR!

"Maybe we should go home," Annie said, quickly jumping up from the porch.

"I think we should check it out," Ben said.

"Didn't Kilmer say that Bruno was in the basement?" Jane asked.

Annie nodded and her eyes got really wide. "What if Bruno ate Hilda, Boris, and Kilmer?"

"Don't be silly," Jane said. "I'm sure that could never happen. At least, I don't think so."

"What if they need help?" Annie asked.

"I know how to find out," Ben said, running over to the basement window.

"You shouldn't spy on our neighbors," Annie scolded.

Ben ignored Annie, stooped down by the basement window, and peered in.

"Maybe Ben is right. We should check on the Hauntlys," Jane said. "Just to make sure they're okay."

Annie nodded and the two girls joined Ben at the basement window. "I can't see anything," Annie complained. "The window is too grimy."

"Shhh," Jane said. "I hear something."

GRRRRRR! HISSSSSS! RROOAARR!

"I don't like the sound of this," Annie whispered. "We should get out of here before it's too late."

"It is already too late," said a voice from behind them. All three kids turned to stare into the crooked yellow teeth of Priscilla Pocus.

6

What a Trick!

"What are my pretty little ones doing?" Priscilla Pocus asked.

Annie gulped, but Jane didn't hesitate. "We were trying to teach Kilmer's spiders to do tricks when we heard horrible noises coming from the basement."

"We thought Kilmer might be in danger from Bruno," Ben told Priscilla.

Priscilla laughed a funny cackling laugh. "Bruno would not hurt my little Kilmer. What is this about teaching spiders tricks?"

"Ben tried to teach them to stand on their heads," Annie explained. "He didn't have any luck."

"Let's take a look at these stubborn spiders," Priscilla suggested. Priscilla glided over to the porch and stared at the glass

cases. She clapped her hands and said a little rhyme:

"Spinning webs and flies don't dread. Now, my sweeties, stand on your head."

"Oh, my gosh," Annie squealed. "It worked! The spiders are actually flipping over."

"That's not all," Jane said to Annie. "Look at Sparky." Sparky came running around the corner of the house and landed on her head. Then she stood up and rubbed Priscilla's leg.

Ben cheered, still watching the spiders. "All right! Just wait until Prissy Issy sees this!"

Annie crossed her arms and looked at Priscilla Pocus. "How did you do that?" Annie asked.

Priscilla smiled, showing her yellow teeth. "It's nothing really," she said. "I just have a way with creatures."

"You sure do," Ben said. "Do you think you could get Minerva to jump into this water?"

Priscilla ran her long green fingernails through her jet-black hair. "One never knows what one can do until one tries," she cackled.

Priscilla took the water bowl out of Minerva's case. She held Minerva in her long bony hand near the water. Priscilla chanted another rhyme.

"Your life is safe in my hand. Jump now upon my command. Into the swirl, my little girl."

Before Ben's eyes Minerva crawled off

Priscilla's hand and fell into Sparky's water bowl.

"That's the coolest trick I've ever seen," Ben said after Priscilla picked Minerva out of the water bowl and put the spider back in her case.

"Look out!" Jane yelled. Sparky leaped over Annie's head and landed right smack dab in the water bowl. Water splashed all over Jane, Annie, and Ben.

"What is wrong with this crazy cat?" Ben asked.

Priscilla just smiled and lifted the dripping cat out of the water. Sparky purred as Priscilla held her close.

GRRRRRRRRR! HISSSSSSS!

"There are those weird sounds again," Jane told Priscilla.

Priscilla smiled. "My sweet Bruno must be nervous. I must go to him." Priscilla gave Sparky one last pat and rushed inside Hauntly Manor Inn.

"Did you see what Priscilla did?" Ben asked his sister. "Wasn't that totally cool?"

But Annie didn't answer Ben. Instead, she put her hand on Ben's shoulder. "I have some bad news for you," she said. "You can't enter the pet show."

7
Homework Spell

"What are you talking about?" Ben asked Annie.

Annie put her hands on her hips. "You can't enter these spiders in the pet show."

"Why not?" Ben asked. "I'm sure to win with the cool tricks they can do."

Annie shook her head. "These spiders have been put under a spell."

"A spell?" Ben and Jane shouted together.

"Annie's flipped her lid." Ben laughed.

"I have not," Annie said, stomping her foot on the Hauntlys' porch. "Didn't you hear Priscilla Pocus saying those weird rhymes?"

Ben and Jane nodded.

Annie pointed her finger at the spiders.

"That was Priscilla casting a spell on those poor little spiders."

Ben laughed. "If that's true, I want Priscilla to go to school with me. Maybe she could put a no-homework spell on my teacher."

Jane laughed, too, and slapped Ben's hand in agreement.

"This is not a joke," Annie said. "Didn't you notice how Priscilla was dressed? What kind of ordinary person goes around dressed totally in black and has weird green fingernails like that?"

Jane shrugged. "My cousin is from New York City and she dresses like that."

"This is not New York," Annie pointed out. "This is Bailey City and here people don't dress like creatures from the black lagoon."

Ben twirled his finger beside his head. "You're crazy. Having these spiders do tricks is the best thing that ever happened around here. You're just jealous because I'm going to win that new bicycle."

262

Annie stomped her foot again. "I'm telling you that Priscilla is dangerous. She is definitely a witch!"

"A witch?" Issy yelled from behind Annie. "Who is a witch?"

Jane jumped up from the porch. There on the sidewalk stood Issy. Her green parrot, Filbert, sat on her shoulder.

"Annie was just kidding around," Jane said. "She might be a witch for next Halloween."

"I thought she called someone named Priscilla a witch," Issy said.

"Jane is just being nice," Ben said. "But I won't be. Annie was calling you a witch!"

Issy's eyes got big. "You were calling *me* a witch?"

Ben folded his arms in front of his chest and nodded, but Annie grabbed Issy's wrist. "Don't get mad," Annie told Issy. "I was just joking."

Issy's face got bright red. "You won't be joking around when I win that new bicycle this weekend."

"You aren't going to win," Ben blurted out, "because I have a secret weapon."

"Shhh," Jane hissed, but it was too late. Issy was already looking at the spider cases.

8

Parrot-Eating Pet

"What are those disgusting little things?" Issy asked.

Ben pulled his shoulders back proudly. "Those are the pet spiders that are going to win the bicycle," he told Issy.

"Ben," Jane warned, "maybe you'd better keep quiet about that."

Issy just laughed and petted the parrot on her shoulder. "There's no way a bunch of bugs can beat my parrot."

"Spiders aren't bugs," Annie explained. "They're arachnids."

"And they are a lot smarter than your pile of stinking feathers. Just watch this," Ben said. Ben looked at the spiders and repeated Priscilla's words:

"Spinning webs and flies don't dread. Now, my sweeties, stand on your head."

As the four kids watched, the spiders flipped over on their heads. Even Sparky stood on her head. Issy's eyes got big and she gasped. "I knew something funny was going on around here. That chant was a magical spell."

Jane shook her head. "It's just a little rhyme that Priscilla Pocus chanted."

"It sounds like hocus pocus to me," Issy said. "Priscilla must have some kind of magical powers. This isn't normal."

"Neither are you," Ben said, "but we still let you hang around."

Issy put her hands on her hips. She started to speak, but the strange noise from Kilmer's basement stopped her short.

GRRRRRRRRR! HISSSSSSSSSSSS!

"Oh, my gosh," Issy squealed, and her pet parrot flapped his wings. "What was that horrible sound?"

Jane patted Issy's shoulder. "Don't worry. It won't hurt you."

"It might eat your parrot, though," Ben

said with an evil laugh. "That's Kilmer's parrot-eating pet."

"What kind of crazy place is this, anyway?" Issy said, her face turning pale. "The people who live here aren't normal."

"Welcome to Hauntly Manor," Boris Hauntly said, coming onto the porch with his wife, Hilda. Issy took one look at Boris' slime-green eyes and Hilda's wild hair and ran screaming down the street. Issy's parrot flapped its wings and perched on a dead tree branch in the Hauntlys' front yard.

"What a strange little girl," Boris said before he and Hilda went back into the house.

Jane grabbed Ben's arm. "We'd better go get Issy."

Ben shook his head. "No way. I'm glad she's gone."

"Don't you understand?" Jane explained. "If we don't get her, she's going to tell everyone that funny things are going on at Hauntly Manor Inn."

"You're right," Annie said. "She might

268

even tell everyone that Kilmer's family is a bunch of monsters."

"What can we do?" Ben asked.

"Don't worry," Annie said. "I have an idea."

9

Secret Weapon

"It won't work," Ben said bluntly after Annie explained her plan. Jane, Annie, and Ben still stood on the Hauntlys' front porch.

"It's kind of mean," Jane said.

Annie shrugged. "We'll only use it like a secret weapon if it's absolutely necessary to protect the Hauntlys and Priscilla from Issy."

"I guess it's worth a try," Jane agreed.

"What do we do first?" Ben asked.

Annie walked over to the Hauntlys' front door. "First, we ask for help," she explained and banged the knocker.

Slowly, the door creaked open. Priscilla Pocus stood in the doorway. Her black dress swirled around her feet and she brushed back her long black hair with green fingernails. "Hello, my pretty little ones," Priscilla said. "What can I do for you?"

"We were hoping you could help us one more time," Annie explained.

Priscilla laughed. It sounded like a witch cackling to Jane and it sent chills up her spine. "Would you like me to teach the spiders another trick?" Priscilla asked.

"Sure," Ben said quickly.

Annie frowned at him and shook her head. "Actually," Annie said, "we were hoping we could teach that parrot to say some funny words."

Priscilla took one look at the bright green parrot sitting on the dead tree limb and smiled. "It will be a pleasure," Priscilla said.

Priscilla pointed to the parrot and curled her finger before saying, *"Feathers flying all around. Come to me, on the ground."*

Immediately, the parrot flew to the porch and landed by Priscilla's feet.

Priscilla patted the parrot's head. "Now, what shall we teach the parrot to say?" Priscilla asked.

Ben grinned. "I have some good ideas about that."

The three kids giggled and Priscilla cackled as they taught the parrot some silly sayings. All it took was a little rhyme from Priscilla and the parrot was squawking anything they wanted him to say.

"This is fantastic," Jane told Priscilla.

"It's wonderful," Annie agreed. "Thank you, Priscilla."

Ben laughed. "I can't wait to see Issy's face when her bird squawks these sayings."

"Hopefully that will never happen," Annie reminded him.

"We better take this bird back to Issy," Jane said.

Annie nodded. "I'll do it," she volunteered. She carefully picked up the parrot and carried it on her arm to Issy's house.

Issy rushed out of the house and grabbed her parrot from Annie. "Oh, Filbert," Issy cried. "I thought I'd never see you again."

"You left him at the Hauntlys'," Annie explained.

Issy buried her face in Filbert's feathers. "I was afraid that crazy family might put him under a magical spell and turn him into a gorilla."

Annie giggled. "The Hauntlys are very nice. They would never do anything like that."

Issy stared at Annie. "The Hauntlys are strange, and if I didn't have to teach Filbert some tricks for tomorrow's pet show, I would do something about it."

10

Operation Parrot

"I'm going to win," Ben sang as he knocked on Kilmer's door. It was the next day and the pet show was only an hour away. Annie and Jane stood next to Ben on the porch. Annie carried a big bowl of water.

"Maybe Kilmer will win," Jane told Ben. "His pet sounds very unusual."

Ben shrugged. "It'll have to be fantastic to beat my acrobatic spiders."

"Those are Kilmer's spiders," Annie reminded him.

"I know," Ben said. "If they win, I'll let Kilmer ride the bicycle, too."

Kilmer opened the door to Hauntly Manor Inn. Kilmer always looked strange, but today he looked worse than usual. His shirt was ripped in several places and his jeans had more holes than a golf course.

"What happened to you?" Jane asked.

"Bruno," Kilmer said as he led his friends into the living room. "Bruno has been most uncooperative. He refuses to wear a leash and he's too big for a cage."

"Oh, my gosh," Annie said when she saw Kilmer's living room. The old couch was turned over and several chairs had the stuffing torn out. "Did Bruno do this?" Annie asked.

Kilmer nodded. "I guess I cannot enter the pet show," he said sadly.

"Why don't you enter Sparky?" Jane suggested.

"No," Kilmer said. "Sparky might eat Eddie's dog."

Ben gulped. "I can't believe I'm saying this. Why don't we share the spiders?"

Kilmer put his hand on Ben's back. "You would do that for me?" Kilmer asked.

"Sure," Ben said with a smile.

"Then let's get going," Jane said. To-

gether the four kids and the three spiders headed off toward Bailey City Park. Annie still carried the big bowl of water. Kilmer's cat, Sparky, trailed along behind.

Bright yellow and green balloons decorated the stage in the middle of the park. A huge sign said: PET SHOW TODAY!

"Look," Jane said. "There's Issy with her parrot."

Issy sat on a park bench beside a girl named Liza. Liza was brushing the hair of a little kitten. Eddie sat on the ground beside a huge Dalmatian. The dog licked Eddie's face.

"It looks like half of Bailey City is here today," Annie said, looking at the crowd of kids around the stage.

"It won't do them any good," Ben said smugly. "Kilmer and I have the pet contest tied up tight."

Finally, the pet show began. Eddie went first and his dog knocked down two of the judges. Liza's kitten was so scared, it jumped on a balloon and popped it. Issy's

parrot sat on Issy's shoulder and said, "Awwk!" Several other kids brought their dogs onto the stage and one kid even had a pet pig. Finally, it was time for the last contestant.

Ben grinned when his name was called. Kilmer and Ben carried the spider cases onto the stage. Annie put the water bowl beside the cases. Sparky sat on the end of the stage, behind Kilmer.

Ben whispered Priscilla's rhyme and waved his hands around.

"Spinning webs and flies don't dread. Now, my sweeties, stand on your head."

The crowd gasped as the spiders stood on their heads. Behind Kilmer's back Sparky stood on her head, too.

Ben smiled and said the other rhyme. Kilmer held Minerva in his hand.

"Your life is safe in my hand. Jump now upon my command. Into the swirl, my little girl."

Minerva crawled to the side of Kilmer's hand and fell into the bowl of water. As

the crowd cheered, Sparky leaped over
Kilmer's back and landed face first into the
bowl. Everyone in the crowd cheered. Ben
groaned. "Sparky, you better not have ru-
ined our chances to win."

"Oh no, my dear boy," said the head
judge. "On the contrary. We've never seen
a better-trained cat. Your cat has won first
place!"

Ben jumped and whooped. "Actually,
it's Kilmer's pet," he said when he finished
cheering.

Kilmer smiled as the judge wheeled out a brand-new shiny red bicycle. The crowd cheered.

"Don't worry," Kilmer told Ben. "We'll share it." Ben grinned and clapped along with the crowd.

One person in the crowd wasn't clapping and that was Issy. Issy was mad. She pushed her way through the crowd and stomped onto the stage.

"Oh, no," Annie said. "I think it's time for Operation Parrot."

11

Filbert Has His Say

Issy marched clear across the stage. Filbert clutched her shoulder, hanging on tight. With each step she took, Filbert's wings fluttered and slapped her on the head. Issy didn't stop until she reached the judge. She grabbed his sleeve and tugged.

The judge glanced down at Issy and her bird. "What seems to be the problem?" he asked.

"You can't give those monsters the prize," she said loud enough for her words to echo over the microphone. "I should get the bike because I worked hard at training Filbert."

"We worked hard, too," Ben said. "We trained Minerva, Elvira, and Winifred."

"But they had help!" Issy interrupted.

The judge scratched his chin. "I believe help is allowed," he told Issy.

"Not the kind of help I saw," she said. "It was definitely not fair."

The rest of the crowd was quiet as they waited for Issy to continue. Annie crossed her fingers and Jane gasped. "Ben better hurry up," Jane said, "before it's too late!"

Issy opened her mouth, but Ben spoke before she had a chance. *"Filbert was there. He knows what to say. He'll tell the truth, and right away!"*

When Ben uttered the words Filbert flapped his wings and hopped onto the judge's shoulder. "Awk!" Filbert screeched over the microphone. "Issy talks too much. Awk!"

The crowd giggled, but Issy's mouth fell open and her ears turned pink.

Filbert didn't notice. He squawked again. "Awk! Issy wears purple underwear. AWK!"

Now Issy's entire face was the color of a raspberry. Before Filbert could say another

word, Issy turned and raced off the stage. Filbert fluttered from the judge's shoulder and flew after her.

The judge looked at Ben and Kilmer. Then he looked at the rest of the audience. "My, my," the judge said. "I guess that bird can talk after all. I think Filbert and Issy deserve second place!"

The audience clapped, but Issy didn't come back to get her prize.

"We'll take the prize to her," Kilmer said. "We know where she lives."

"Thank you," the judge said. "But first, it's time for us to give you and Sparky your prize."

The crowd cheered as the judge gave Kilmer the shiny red bicycle.

"Wow," Ben said. "That is the coolest bicycle I've ever seen!"

Kilmer didn't say a word, but he definitely did not look happy.

12
Kilmer Makes a Deal

Ben was up early the next morning. He raced over to Hauntly Manor Inn on his old bicycle. Annie and Jane had to hurry to keep up with him.

Ben's bike used to be shiny black, but now it was covered with scratches and dents. He dropped his bike in the dead grass right next to Kilmer's new red one parked in front of the inn.

"I'm going to see if Kilmer wants to go riding," Ben said. "Maybe he'll let me ride his new bike."

Annie grabbed Ben's arm before he had a chance to knock on the door. "Are you sure Kilmer knows how to ride?"

"Of course he does," Ben snapped. "Everybody knows how to ride a bike."

"Don't be so sure," Jane said. "After all,

Kilmer didn't act too happy about it yesterday. He didn't even smile and he rolled his bike all the way home."

"Maybe he just felt bad about Issy," Annie said. "She really was embarrassed in front of everybody."

"We had to do it," Ben said, "before she told everybody about Priscilla Pocus. Besides, I think she felt better when we gave her the second place prize."

"I guess you're right," Annie said. "But Kilmer didn't try riding his new bike once."

"That's because we had our hands full," Ben said. That was true. The kids had to carry home the spiders and water bowl. "Kilmer's new bike is the best, and I'll prove it."

Before the girls could say another word, Ben lifted the giant tarnished door knocker and let it fall. They heard heavy footsteps echoing through Hauntly Manor Inn. Then the door slowly squeaked open and Kilmer peered out at them.

Ben smiled. "How about a bike ride?" he asked.

Kilmer shrugged, but he still didn't look very happy.

"Don't you like your new bike?" Annie asked.

Kilmer sighed. "It is a nice bike," he said sadly.

"Then what's wrong?" Jane asked.

Kilmer looked past his three friends and out into the yard. He smiled when he saw Ben's bike. "I just wish my bike were more like Ben's."

"WHAT?" Annie said. "His bike is scratched up."

"And full of dents," Jane added.

"Yes," Kilmer said. "It is the best-looking bike in Bailey City."

Jane, Annie, and Ben looked at each other and shrugged. "If you really like my bike better," Ben said with a grin, "I'll trade with you."

"Do you mean it?" Kilmer asked. "You would really take my new bike and let me have your black one?"

Ben shrugged. "Sure. After all, we are friends."

Kilmer jumped up and yelled. When he landed, the entire porch shook. "It's a deal," Kilmer said.

Just then, Sparky darted out the door. She skidded to a stop and arched her back. With her ears plastered back against her head, she hissed at Jane, Annie, and Ben. Then Sparky raced down the steps and disappeared around the corner of the house.

"I think Priscilla needs to remind Sparky to be friendly," Annie joked.

Kilmer shook his head. "Priscilla left last night," he said. "She likes to fly when there is a full moon. That way she can see better."

Then Kilmer followed Ben down the steps and they both hopped on their bicycles. Annie and Jane watched Ben race away on the shiny red bike. Kilmer followed him on the scarred black bike.

"I guess the magic spell is gone," Annie said. "It flew away with Priscilla."

"At least everything is back to normal," Jane said.

Annie pointed at the ground. Three hairy spiders crawled out of the inn and slowly climbed on Jane's sneaker. "With the Hauntlys as neighbors," Annie said, "things may never be normal again."

About the Authors

Marcia Thornton Jones and **Debbie Dadey** like to write about monsters. Their first series with Scholastic, **The Adventures of the Bailey School Kids**, has many characters who are *monsterously* funny. Now with the Hauntly family, Marcia and Debbie are in monster heaven!

Marcia and Debbie both used to live in Lexington, Kentucky. They were teachers at the same elementary school. Recently, Debbie and her family moved to Fort Collins, Colorado. Marcia and her husband still live in Kentucky, where she continues to teach. How do these authors write together? They talk on the phone and use computers and fax machines!